MONSTERS
FATED ENCOUNTERS

MONSTERS
FATED ENCOUNTERS

D.R. Mills

SEA OF INK PRESS

MONSTERS
FATED ENCOUNTERS

Cover art: MiblArt
Interior book design: Enchanted Ink Publishing
Illustrations: Gabrielle Ragusi
Editing: A. P. Mobley at Sea of Ink Press

ISBN: 978-1-7358479-7-9 (Paperback)

Thank you for your support of the author's rights.

SEA OF INK PRESS

For my wife

Meeting you was chance.
Loving you was fate.

D.R. MILLS
PRESENTS . . .

MONSTERS

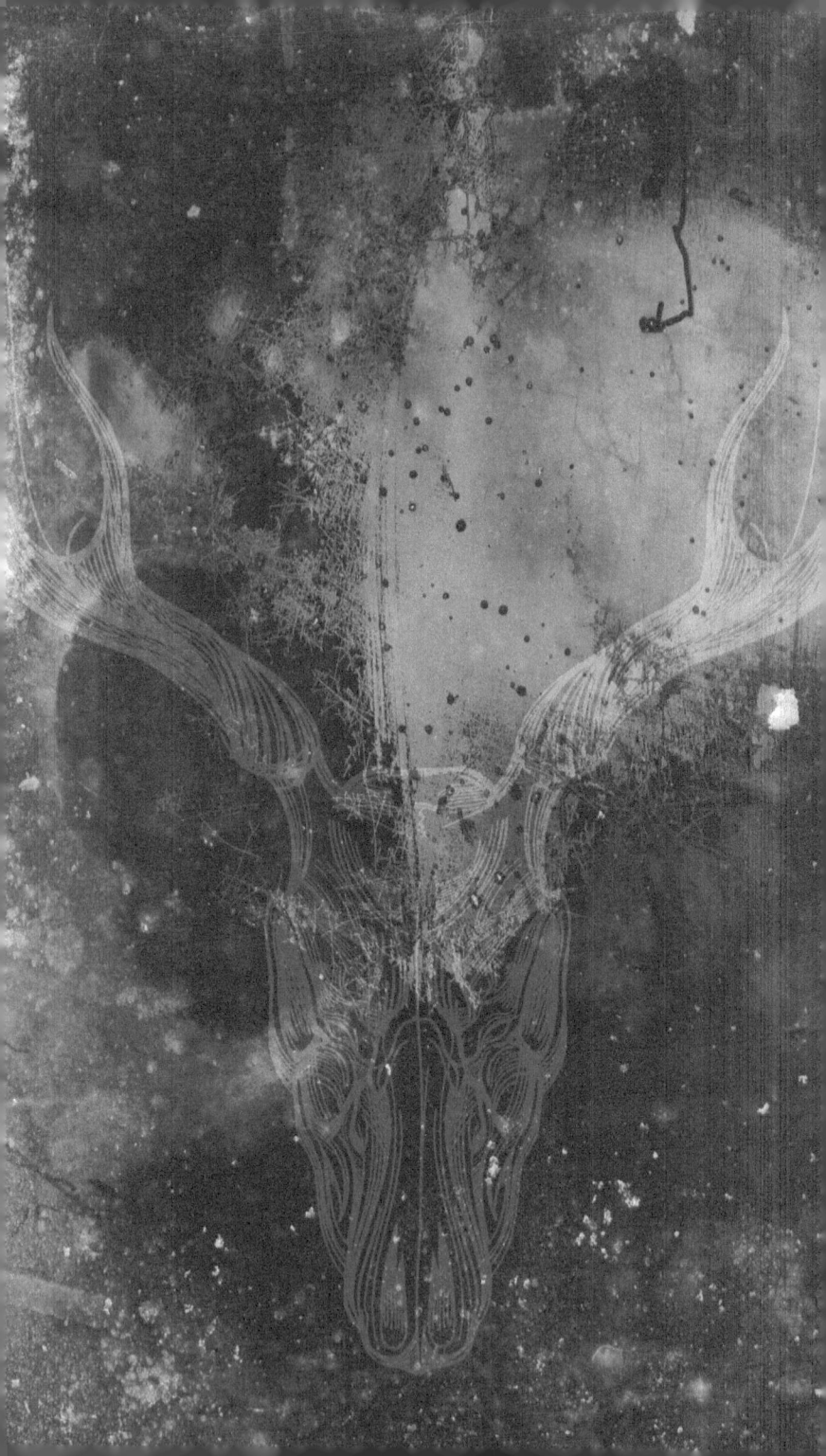

*G*ENTLE SNOWFALL BLANKETED THE NIGHT sky, the moonlight overhead making the near-frozen surface of Donner Lake sparkle. It was a truly beautiful sight in Magnus Myers's opinion.

Magnus parked his dark-blue truck in an open space in the parking lot. He let the engine die and allowed the vehicle to settle for a moment before opening the door and stepping out into the cold winter air.

It was a windless, cloudless night for Donner Village, and after such a long drive with the heater on full blast, Magnus felt oddly relaxed by the icy bite outside. He took another look at the shining lake before him, then turned and walked across the asphalt, toward the hotel lobby.

The bell above the door jingled as Magnus entered. Directly across from the main entrance sat the front desk. It remained unoccupied, but a woman's voice called from somewhere within the office behind it, "I'll be with you in a second!" Magnus tilted his head, trying to catch a glimpse of whoever the voice belonged to, but saw no one. *Guess I have a little time to look around*, he thought.

Chairs had been placed near the spacious lobby's front door, a small magazine rack standing next to them. What appeared to be a kind of lounge area beckoned from the far-left side of the room. It featured a fireplace, a television, and two couches.

However, Magnus wasn't here to relax. He was here on business. He scanned the other side of the room and spotted a wooden board filled with missing persons posters. *There they are.*

He ambled over to the board, examining the faces of everyone lost. All the placards had similar wording; they said these folks had gone missing within the past three weeks. There were a few younger women, a couple of older men. Multiple children of both genders. All of them last seen leaving the ski resort or somewhere near Donner Pass.

Magnus stared hard at their faces. *These poor people...* He knew they were more than just "missing." That's what he had been told, anyway.

The sound of heels clacking against wooden flooring ripped his attention away from the wall of faces and back toward the front desk. A stout woman in a white-and-blue blouse stepped out of the office and greeted him with a warm smile. "Hi! Welcome to the Donner Inn. How can I help you?"

"I need a room for a couple of nights," Magnus said, returning her friendly tone.

She nodded and took a seat at the desk, then began typing away at her computer. After a moment, she looked back up at him and smiled again. "You're just in time. I have one room left."

"Great. Just put it on here, please." He pulled out his wallet and handed her a credit card. She took the card and swiped it through a reader next to the computer. As she worked, Magnus took another glance at the board nearby. "Lots'a folks going missing around here lately, huh?"

"Oh, yeah," she said, her wide eyes never leaving the computer screen. "It's kinda weird."

"How so?" Magnus asked.

"Well," she began, finally facing him, "there are just so many similar cases in such a short amount of time. And the police haven't found anything. No bodies, no evidence to say where the people have gone. It's super creepy." She leaned in and whispered, "I had one guy in here the other day saying it was a series of alien abductions."

She returned his card, and Magnus chuckled. "Yeah, I don't know about that one," he said, then returned the card to his wallet and slipped that into his pocket. "But I mean, hey, who knows? The truth is stranger than fiction, right?"

"That's for sure," she replied with a laugh. She printed a receipt and handed Magnus a room key. "You'll be up in room 237. Just head up the stairs on the right, and it's down the hall on the left. There's a laundry room and snack and soda machines across from you if you'll be needing anything like that. Otherwise, there's a diner open 24-7 not too far down the street."

Magnus nodded and turned to leave. "Thanks. Have a good night, and be safe."

"You, too." She returned to her office as Magnus exited the lobby and walked toward his truck. *Truth certainly is stranger than fiction*, he thought. *If only they knew what was really happening to those poor people.*

He opened the back seat door and grabbed two bags, the faces of every missing person on that wooden board flashing through his mind like a deck of cards being shuffled at a rapid pace. Matching posters for his daughter, Paige, and his grandson, Ryan, made appearances in the mix, although they hadn't been lost. The thought of Paige and Ryan being hurt in the same manner those folks had made Magnus's drive to stop the monster ever stronger, though.

He closed the door and headed toward the tailgate. Once he opened it, he grabbed his duffel bag from inside. A quick tug on the bag's zipper revealed his big, pure-silver knife. The blade remained sheathed and lay atop his other weapons and gear. He zipped up the bag, pulled it out, and threw it over his shoulder, then slammed the tailgate shut. *I've got to find this thing and stop it before anybody else gets hurt.*

He returned to the lobby and started up the stairs to the right. It didn't take long to reach his room. He used the key to open the door, then stepped inside.

There was a bathroom on his right, and ahead of him a king-sized bed with crisp, clean sheets sat before a medium-sized TV. There was also a second room next to the bed, which housed a fireplace, a mini fridge, and a table with a coffee pot.

Magnus walked over to the bed and rested his bags on it. *What I don't understand is how the monster is moving from areas that are so far away from each other at such a rapid pace*, he thought. *How did it kidnap somebody up on the mountain, but also take somebody down in Donner Pass with short intervals between the abductions?*

It certainly was puzzling. Which creatures even had that kind of maneuverability? He shook his head and took a moment to remove his boots, then strolled into the second part of his room and glanced out the window. The view of Donner Lake, of its bright surface, was absolutely breathtaking. The reflections of the moonlight and the snowfall created a gentle gleam that shimmered against the ceiling above him.

He looked down at his forearm, at the faded tattoo of the black eye just above his elbow. Memories of the past few months flooded his mind, and with them came a deep, empty pit in his stomach. He clenched his jaw, then lowered his arm and turned back to the window.

I can't fail this town like I failed Twilight Peak.

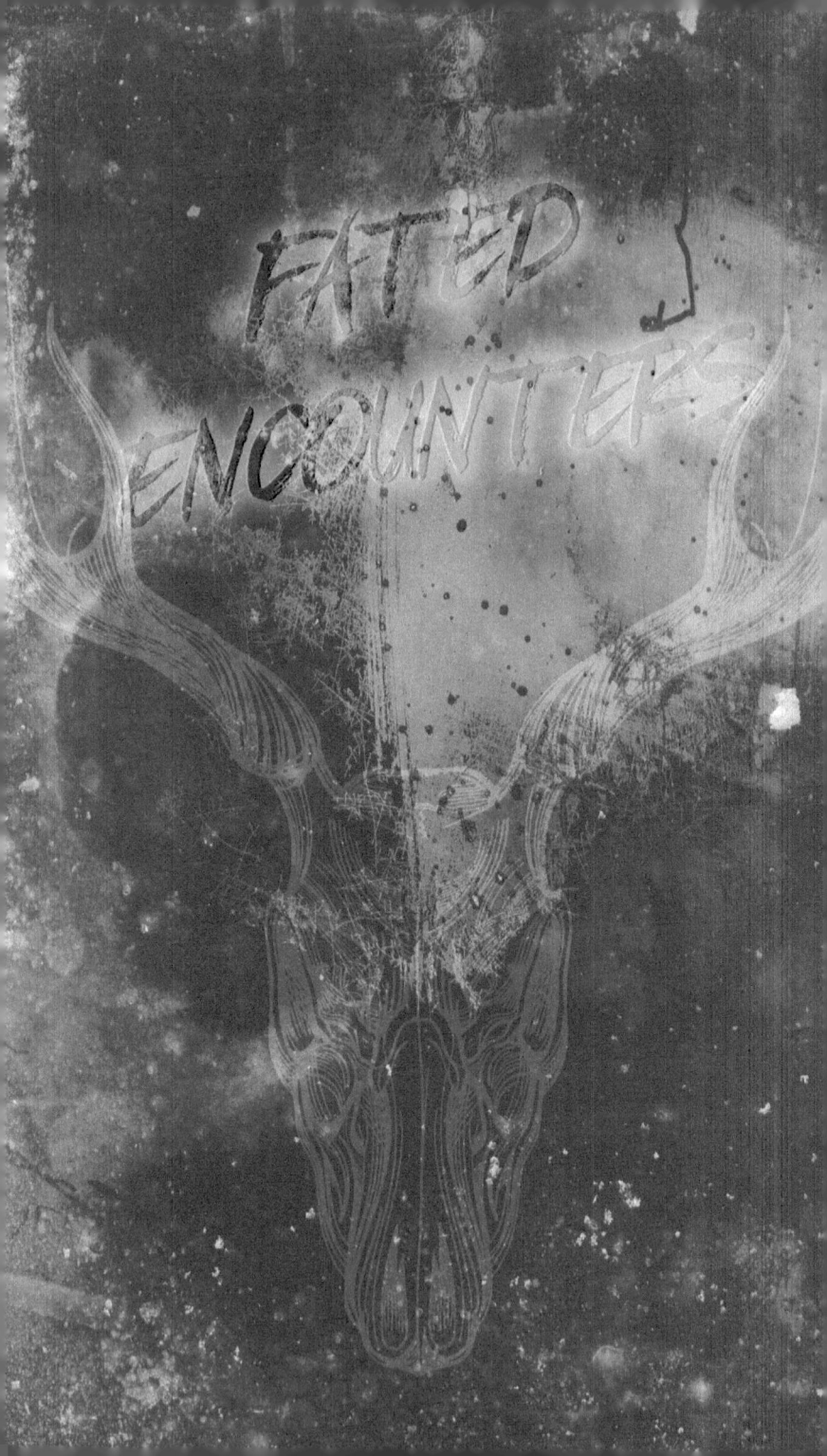

CHAPTER 1

MONTRA BOS SEARCHED THE SNOW.

It was early morning and the sun had yet to rise, but his kind possessed excellent vision in the dark. The icy layer covering the grass chilled his feet. It didn't bother him much, though. He knelt and inspected the ground. Most of the brush that managed to poke out of the snow wasn't anything too... Ah, this could be it.

A healthy bramble, freshly sprouted from the earth, thrived here despite the frigid winter temperatures. That could only mean one thing. Montra shuffled on all fours toward the bramble and began digging in the snow below it. It took a while for him to find what he was searching for, but eventually he discovered it.

Bones had been strewn across a pile of frozen hide. After pulling and digging a bit more, he managed to loosen some of the larger bones. He took them in his hands and examined them. It was hard to say what kind of creature they belonged to, but his best guess was a woodswalker. Woodswalkers always provided for the needs of the village.

"I'm surprised," a voice called from behind. Montra turned to find Father standing on the nearby hillside. Atwa Brava's fur was a darker brown than Montra's, and his bright-orange stripes rounded up and around his arms and waist. "I figured you'd be down by the man-villages rather than out here searching for takes." His father slid down the hill, balancing himself on the slippery surface with his tail as he approached Montra.

"Natwa is showing me how to make my own dagger," Montra admitted.

"Aye," Father said, nodding. "He told me before I came looking for you." The look in his deep-yellow eyes and the tone of his voice told Montra there was a lecture coming, and it didn't surprise him. His father rested his hands on Montra's shoulders. "You know you shouldn't be out here alone."

"Aye," Montra replied, holding his father's gaze.

"I'm more than happy to escort you, my son. Why didn't you ask me?"

"Mother needs you." And it was true. Montra's mother had recently given life to his little sister not yet two moons ago, and she needed more support than ever to give the child proper care. "Natwa would have come, but I didn't ask him," he continued. "I wanted to be alone."

His father sighed and squeezed his shoulders. "Our kind is dying, Montra. There is evil out here with us. We can't risk anyone else being lost."

Montra nodded and looked to the ground. He paused before speaking again. "Is it men that kill our kind?" His father didn't answer right away. He glanced up to find a troubled expression on the older Ooawan's face.

"Do not worry about that right now," Father finally said. "Did you get what you need?" Montra nodded and held up the bones he dug up. "Then let us return home. It's not safe to be this far from the village alone." He lowered a hand to Montra's back and gently pushed him in the direction of the village. Together, they started up the hill.

The answer Montra had received, or, rather, the answer he *hadn't* received, bothered him. He knew how his father felt about men and their ways. Atwa's opinion of the creatures who destroyed and disrespected nature was as low as you would expect, and if men were indeed behind the recent killings, wouldn't he just say so? Montra had always been interested in men--their possessions, their ways. He even found the cloths they wore on their naked bodies fascinating.

Is Father afraid of telling me the truth because he knows how I feel about them? Montra had been caught and taken home just like today on many occasions, only he'd normally been found outside of man-dwellings and -villages. But this morning was different. Several dead Ooawans had been found in the past few days. Montra didn't know much about the deaths other than something seemed to be hunting his people. His father and many of the others back home were frightened, and Montra had never known his father to be afraid of anything. After all, Atwa was the Village Leader.

"You're scared," Montra said after a long silence. "If it were men, I don't think you would be. It's something else."

His father let the thought hang in the air before answering. "Everyone is scared. Your mother, Sina, and yes, even I. There has not been something like this in…" He trailed off as though deep in thought. "Why, it would have to have been after our ancestors' earliest encounters with men."

"Can we not fight?" Montra asked. "Surely if we stop what's hurting our kind--"

"The force responsible cannot be fought, my son," Father interrupted, his tone forceful. "We would only lose more lives if we tried."

Montra huffed. His breath clouded the air around his nostrils, then faded away. "So you *do* know what it is."

"Aye," his father admitted. "I do. And it might be better for the village if we leave our home to find safety elsewhere."

Montra stopped in his tracks and bared his teeth. "What?" His father made a movement surely meant to calm him, but he paid it no mind. "We can't abandon our home! Our village has stood here for lifetimes."

"I know," Father said. "I like the idea even less than you, but it might be our only option."

"If you don't like the idea, then why consider it?"

"Because it has worked for us before. Our kind once lived farther down the mountain. But, as man expanded, we were forced to move. That happened often." Montra relaxed, easing his stance. "This may be the only home you and I have ever known," Father continued as he resumed walking, "but our ancestors were faced with this very same decision, and we are alive today because of their choices."

Montra followed, letting his tail drag along the ground. The idea of leaving the forest and terrain he knew so well... made him feel ill. The world beyond the mountains they called home was dangerous. Where else could they possibly go that would be safer? How was this fair?

Light began to shine and split through the trees behind them, the sun finally rising. Montra followed his father in silence until they arrived in the village. Huts made of broad branches and various fauna hides came into view, smoke curling out from the tops of a few of them.

His father walked him to the front of their family's hut, a large one near the center of the village. "Hurry inside and check on your mother," Father instructed. "I must begin preparations for the Naming Ceremony tonight."

Montra nodded as his father turned and walked off. He stood for a moment, looking down to the bones in his hand. *Can we really not fight this threat? How dangerous can it be?* Before he could think of an explanation, a familiar scent found its way into his nose. He turned to see his older brother, Natwa, approaching him from the opposite direction he and Father had come from.

"Hello, Brother," Natwa said. "Father was searching for you, and I thought you to still be asleep." Natwa carried a hefty piece of timber on his shoulders that had two water buckets suspended on each end. He gently set the timber down as he arrived at Montra's side. "Are you well?"

Montra nodded. "Aye." He held up the bones for Natwa to see. "I found these down by Two Trees." Natwa took the bones from Montra's open palm and began examining them with his intense yellow eyes.

Natwa Bes represented everything Ooawan culture stood for. He was considerate of his customs, caring for his people, and always willing to help the village. He was also strong, nimble, and an excellent hunter. It wouldn't surprise anyone if, once his father passed, he became the next Village Leader. He even shared the same shade of brown fur as his father, as well as a similar pattern of orange stripes on his back.

Natwa hummed as he inspected the bones. "These might not be the best ones to use for your dagger, but they will work for now." Montra couldn't help but feel disappointed. He didn't want to compete with Natwa, but he always felt like his older brother was better at everything. Any time he gained Natwa's approval, it felt like a massive accomplishment. "What creature did you take these from?" Natwa asked.

"I think it was a woodswalker," Montra answered.

Natwa held up the bones to inspect them in the light. "These are big enough to use, I suppose, but they might not be strong enough. Woodswalkers have good hind legs, so be sure to look for those next time."

Montra motioned at the water buckets. "Are these for Mother?"

"Aye," Natwa replied. "Help me take them in, and then we'll get to work on your dagger, if you'd like."

"Yes, I would." Montra rolled the bones up into his tail, then bent over and grabbed one of the pails. Natwa took the other, and together they entered the hut.

The interior felt toasty warm, a noticeable difference from outside. At the back of the hut, seated upon a bed of cloth and grass, was their mother. Sel Ratwa held Montra and Natwa's unnamed baby sister, cooing to the infant. Sel's fur was a tad longer than her two sons', which resulted in a fluffier look than most Ooawans' coats, and hers had always been the lightest in the family. She also sported white stripes rather than orange ones, and the cub had similar stripes to hers. However, the infant didn't only look like her mother. She also had the dark-brown fur of her father.

Mother smiled warmly as they entered with the water in hand. "Hello, my sons," she whispered. "Early man-watching again, Montra?"

"Actually, I was collecting bones, Mother," Montra said. She shook her head as the boys set the water pails next to her, and then Montra knelt down to see the baby. The little one slept soundly in a swaddle of cloth, slowly clenching and unclenching her tiny hands. "How is she?" he asked.

"Healthy," Mother answered. "She's survived her first week without so much as a cough."

"She's strong, like the rest of her family," Natwa said proudly, then patted Montra on the back. Montra looked up at him, and he motioned at the bones Montra still held with his tail. "Let's get your dagger made, aye?"

Montra rose. "Aye."

Together, the brothers stepped away from their mother and sister and walked toward their beds, which were placed opposite to one another. Montra retrieved the other materials for the knife and followed Natwa out of the hut.

Natwa led Montra to the edge of the village, all the way to their favorite spot--Nete-lat Rock, a massive boulder located a ways up the mountain. Nete-lat Rock jutted out of a cliffside and offered a nice view of the village and surrounding trees, and Montra and Natwa often sat upon it when they spent time together.

It took a while for them to run all the way up there, but the trip wasn't difficult because they made it almost every day. Once they stood upon Nete-lat Rock, the brothers sat down, and Montra spread out the materials for his new weapon.

Natwa seized the bones and placed them in Montra's hands. "Snap the largest one in half. It's going to be part of the handle." Montra followed Natwa's instructions, then handed the two halves to his brother. "Now you need to get the thread and wrap, and then…" Natwa trailed off as he took the stone that would act as the blade and positioned it alongside the rest of the items on the ground, forming the incomplete dagger. "You place everything together like this and wrap it very tightly. You want it to be sturdy, so it isn't breaking right away when you use it."

Montra nodded and grabbed up the wrappings. He began to tie everything together as instructed. Moments of silence passed as he worked, Natwa watching. Finally, Montra sighed. "The Naming Ceremony is tonight."

Natwa smiled. "Our little sister will finally have something we can call her by."

"It's an event to look forward to."

Montra hadn't hidden the hesitant tone in his voice as well as he'd wanted to, and Natwa seemed to catch it. "Something troubles you?" he asked.

Montra inserted the next piece of bone to form what would be the handle, then began tying it in with the rest. "So much has happened since she was born…"

Natwa sighed. "Things have been… difficult."

"Father says we might leave to find a new home."

"Aye, he told me that yesterday."

"And you are fine with it?"

"Of course I'm not," Natwa said with a huff. "But the call is not mine to make. It's Father's. He is our

Village Leader, just like his father before him. I trust Father to make the right decision, as should you."

Montra inserted the next piece of bone into the handle and wrapped it. "Aye... I should. I should trust him, but I just... I'm not ready to leave home. It greatly upsets me that everyone else seems so resigned to do so."

Natwa patted Montra on the shoulder. "I understand, Brother. I'd rather stay here as well, believe me, but there's nothing that can be done. Our kind is being killed, and so long as our blood is senselessly shed, this place is not safe."

Montra stayed quiet as he continued to work. He didn't know what else to say. Natwa was right, as always. It was the job of their father to look after the village, even if it meant leaving the land they loved. So why did the idea of doing so still make him feel so... ashamed?

He finished the tie, leaving it loose near the top. "Good work," Natwa said. "Now insert the stone for the blade, tighten that tie, and wrap it."

Montra did as he was told, sliding the stone into place. The tip and edges had been sharpened severely. He grabbed the last bit of fabric and cross-wrapped it around the hilt and blade. Once it was strained and firm, Montra lifted up the finished product for his brother to see.

Natwa snatched the dagger and pointed it around. He gave it a shake, and Montra noticed the blade jiggle slightly. "You see that, too?" Natwa asked.

"Aye," Montra said with a grunt, his nostrils flaring.

"The tying is well-done, Brother. The lack of sturdiness comes from the weaker bones you used." Natwa stood and swung the weapon through the air a few times. He looked it over as Montra climbed to his feet as well. "It's sturdy enough, though. It will hold decently for now." Natwa handed the dagger back to Montra. "Look for better bones to use in the future, but for your first try, this is good."

Montra grasped the dagger and smiled slyly. "Better than your first one, Brother?"

Natwa chuckled. "In a way, yes. I had a great set of bones to use, but my blade wasn't very big. It was better suited to be used as an arrow rather than a knife."

Montra laughed and glanced down at his work. *My first dagger.* Pride swelled in his heart as he looked over its details. Obviously, it was far from perfect, but it had gained Natwa's approval. That was enough for Montra.

It was a short-lived victory, though. Montra's ears drooped as he recalled the discussion they'd just had.

Natwa rested a hand on Montra's shoulder. "Have faith. Things will unfold as the Elder Spirits intend them to. And who knows? Perhaps an even better home than these hills awaits us."

"Perhaps…" Montra mumbled.

"Focus on the Naming Ceremony. Let us look to the good times for now." Montra nodded, and Natwa let go of him and began the descent toward the village.

"Perhaps there isn't anywhere else for us to go, though…" Montra whispered to himself as he watched his brother walk away.

*M*AGNUS STROLLED DOWN a snow-covered street. Donner Village in the early morning was somehow even more beautiful than Donner Village in the late evening. The snowfall had ceased, but it had left a fresh blanket of cold white fluff covering the town.

Magnus was about a block away from his hotel, but instead of going back to his room, he turned left and entered the West Side Diner. A bell chimed overhead as he swung the door open. He stood in the entryway and allowed the door to shut, scanning the diner's interior. It seemed cozy, with dark-brown leather booths and clean white tables, and it smelled of maple syrup and fresh pancakes. Breakfast did sound good, but first he had to find somebody.

Finally, he spotted a man seated alone at a booth in a far-off corner of the building. *There he is.*

Magnus walked past tables of families and what he assumed were regular, everyday customers, then sat down across from the man in the corner booth. "Sorry I'm late, Douglas," he began. "I was enjoying the scenery on my way here."

Magnus considered the man sitting before him an old friend, and any hunter who knew anything knew Douglas Creed. Douglas and Magnus had hunted monsters here and there throughout the years, but their most recent excursion had been when a creature Douglas had been tracking moved into Twilight Peak.

Douglas was stout, stood nearly the same height as Magnus, and had a short ash-gray beard, his irises a deep chocolate brown. He had a slight Australian accent that was fading from his years in the states, and he wore a comfy winter coat and a raccoon-skin cap today.

He smirked at Magnus, then took a sip from his coffee mug. "Nice place, huh?"

Magnus nodded. "Reminds me of home…" He gestured at the cup after a pause. "The coffee any good?"

"Best coffee you'll find this far out of Wyoming," Douglas said tiredly. "Speaking of," he started, then stopped to take another drink. "How is Twilight Peak?"

Magnus ran a hand over his bald head. "It's, uhh… it's been better." Douglas said nothing. He only raised a brow in response.

A waitress approached the table and snapped Magnus from his thoughts. "Hi, what can I get for you?" she asked.

Magnus looked up at her. "Coffee, please. Maybe a menu too?"

"Coming right up." The waitress smiled, then strutted back toward the kitchen.

Once she was out of earshot, Magnus turned to Douglas. "So, you have some details you want to share? You were pretty vague over the phone the other night."

"What do you already know?" Douglas asked.

"Well," Magnus began, "I know there haven't been vanishings like this in the past thirty years. That is, no bodies found, none of the victims heard from again. Usually between ten to twenty people before the disappearances stop. They're just far enough apart that most folks probably don't question them too much."

"Mhmm," Douglas agreed.

Magnus leaned closer. "You said you know what's causing this?"

Douglas raised a finger and pointed it at Magnus. "That I do, mate." He lowered his arm and finished his coffee. "But that can wait until after breakfast. For now, let's worry about how we're gettin' up that mountain."

Magnus sighed. Breakfast did sound pretty good.

CHAPTER 2

MAGNUS HIKED BEHIND DOUGLAS, THE chilly afternoon wind biting his cheeks as he examined the trees. Birds chirped and tweeted, flying between bits of foliage and into the sky.

He sighed contentedly. The fresh air and the sounds of nature relaxed him. In fact, he couldn't remember the last time he'd felt so at peace. It made him miss home.

"So, quite a few of the folks that've turned up missing were experienced hikers," Douglas said. "The kinds of people that grew up around these parts. The kinds of people that don't just 'get lost' out here."

Magnus stepped over a snow-covered log blocking the path, "What is it we're dealing with, then?"

"Somethin' different," Douglas replied as he stopped and turned around to face Magnus. He pulled off his backpack and the rifle he'd slung over his shoulder, then began digging through the open pockets. "A few big-game hunters in the area told me some stories about the creatures they've seen in these woods. Tall, dark fur, weapons fashioned from stones." He offered Magnus a smile, then shook his head and chuckled. "Monsters makin' tools. Freakin' diabolical." He refocused on his bag. "I was close to callin' all of 'em crazy until one of 'em gave me this."

Douglas handed a photo to Magnus. Magnus took it and inspected it beneath the sun.

The image had been captured in a wooded area, not at all unlike the one they currently stood in. However, Magnus had to look over the photo twice before he finally noticed a hidden figure within the picture. It was a humanoid blur of brown, and it stood behind a tree on the far-left side of the photo. Two glowing yellow orbs hovered where its eyes should have been, barely visible beneath the shade the creature was hiding under.

"Spooky, right?" Douglas said. He tapped the photo. "Before you ask, I looked into it. Picture isn't edited at all. Whatever is nestled behind that tree is 100 percent real."

Magnus didn't know what to say. He had faced a plethora of evil spirits and creatures in his time. Repeat encounters with familiar enemies? Simple enough. But discovering a new kind of monster? Now *that* was something else. The more he stared at the photo, the more he started to catch the little details hidden in the shadows. He squinted, peering closer to confirm what he was seeing. Yes, pointed ears--the ears of a feline--topped the creature's head, and now it was impossible to unsee them. "That thing looks like some kind of cat," Magnus said, handing the photo back to Douglas.

"Right you are." Douglas swiped the picture and returned it to his bag. "And whatever this cat-thing is, I'm almost positive it's the monster nabbin' people."

Magnus cupped his chin. "There isn't much to suggest that the cat's the culprit. We don't have any bodies to see how the monster's killing folks, or even *if* it's killing folks."

Douglas let out a sound of disagreement and threw his bag and rifle back over his shoulder. "How many cases you done that you've had less to go off'a?" he asked, and Magnus shrugged. "Exactly. This thing was caught on camera just before the first hiker went missin' a couple'a months ago." He shifted his stance and leaned in close. "There ain't much to look at here, I know that, but this thing poppin' up just before people start vanishin' don't seem like a coincidence to me."

"Why would it take people?" Magnus asked. "For food?"

Douglas smirked. "From the sounds of it, the thing's a bit of a hunter. Wouldn't surprise me if that was the case." He turned and began heading farther into the trees. "We hike in, find where it's hidin', and put it down."

Magnus let out a long exhale as he followed Douglas. "We've got a lot of ground to cover. This thing took people from the area near the ski lodge *and* from Donner Pass. Any idea how to pin it down?"

"Not a clue," Douglas answered, laughing. "But I figure it's pretty mobile if it's movin' around that much. The area between might be where it's hidin' out, so I say we start there."

Douglas's suggestion seemed logical, but for some reason, Magnus felt that the situation was... off. It was as if you had a puzzle piece that featured the missing part of the picture, but when you tried to insert said piece into its rightful place, you found it was the wrong shape and didn't fit at all. *Maybe it's just that we're dealing with a creature unlike anything I've seen before*, Magnus thought.

He didn't bother sharing his concerns with Douglas, though. Not yet, at least. After all, maybe Douglas was right. Maybe this cat-creature was taking people somewhere and killing them.

For now, Magnus would have to hike on to find out.

THE AFTERNOON SHIFTED to evening as the sun began to set, the smell of smoke thick in the air. All around Montra, the Ooawans danced and made merry as a bonfire raged in the center of the village. The Naming Ceremony had begun.

Every new life that came into the village was to be named this way, as was tradition. The flames would burn high, and the Ooawans would celebrate until just before the sun dipped below the horizon. In that brief moment, the Village Elder would give the child his or her true name. Naming Ceremonies were already important to the village, but this one was even more special because it was being held for the daughter of the Village Leader.

As friends and family bounced and spun around Montra, he stood still and watched the fire. It was difficult to feel as jovial as everyone else when he knew what was coming.

A pair of arms suddenly wrapped around his neck, and someone jumped onto his back. He stumbled slightly before catching himself, a female giggling in his ear. "Shouldn't you be celebrating as well, Montra?" she asked, and he immediately recognized who she was.

He snorted. "Aye, I should be..." He dropped her off his back and turned to face her.

Vuli Reywa remained one of the only Ooawans in the village close to Montra's age. Her fur was just a shade lighter than his, but she had additional patches of black as well--most notably a tuft of darkness on the top of her head that was longer than the rest of her coat, which often hung over her eyes. However, her most striking feature had to be her tail. Its fur was far lengthier than anyone else's and was incredibly bushy, which made it appear quite a bit larger than it actually was.

Vuli smiled and tilted her head. Montra couldn't help but notice she wore an artifact that had been passed down from her previous village's Elder, a type of necklace made from shiny metals with a bright-red gem set in the center. "Why do you seem so down?" she asked.

Montra lowered his gaze. He often felt nervous meeting her eyes for long periods of time. It made him even more nervous to tell her that they might have to leave their home and find a new one. "I suppose I'm sad for the lives we've lost recently," he answered.

Vuli's grin vanished. "Aye, it doesn't seem fair they couldn't join us today." Montra already regretted saying anything at all. Her entire demeanor had shifted. This was a scary subject for her, especially since her father, Belta Sen, had been out with the hunting party for days. The thought that he might not come home probably terrified her.

However, she sprang back to life a moment later. She began prancing around Montra. "But let us not speak of that now. Tonight is for celebration!" She seized his hands and hopped up and down, trying to get him to mimic her motions.

Montra laughed, joining in on her jumping. "You're right. We should talk about happier things."

"What of men?" Vuli asked, then stopped suddenly, her eyes widening. "Did you learn anything new on your last trip to their villages?"

Montra shook his head sadly. Vuli was the only other Ooawan he knew that found humans as interesting as he did, and they often discussed men's strange ways together. Journeying down to the man-villages proved more difficult for her, however. Her father was rather strict about where she was allowed to go.

She leaned back and sighed. "What were you out searching for all morning, then?"

"Bones," Montra replied matter-of-factly. "For my dagger."

Vuli huffed but kept her smile. "That is rather important, I suppose. How is it?"

"Loose. But good for a first try."

"So, not as good as mine was?"

"Of course not." This response produced a chuckle out of them both, and then there came an awkward silence as Montra looked down and realized he still held her hands in his. His face grew warm. Maybe it was just because of the fire…

"My people, young and old!" Montra's father called from nearby. The celebration halted as the sky dimmed, and every Ooawan in attendance turned to see Atwa Brava as he stood atop the Ceremony Stand at the head of the village. "Thank you for joining my family at this special time. Night is about to take hold. As is tradition"--he turned and offered a hand to someone behind him--"I'd like to welcome Sina Weltoo, our Village Elder." Another Ooawan wrapped in hides inched her way toward Montra's father. Two other villagers assisted her until Father helped her up onto the stand.

Sina lowered her hood. Her hairless, wrinkled skin was a pale pink, with small dark blotches scattered on her neck. She scanned the crowd with dull-gray eyes, although Montra knew she couldn't actually see anyone because she was blind. "Today," she began, "we gather to ask the Elder Spirits for a child's true name, as we once did for all of you."

Montra watched as his mother approached Sina, carrying the baby. Despite Sina's blindness, her ear twitched at the sound of Mother's steps, and she turned. Mother stopped next to Sina, and Sina placed a gentle hand upon the baby's forehead, then lifted her other arm toward the sky as if searching for something. The baby stirred, perhaps uncomfortable or afraid.

Suddenly Sina gasped. She threw her head back and struggled for air. Thankfully, though, it didn't take long for her breathing to return to normal. She lowered her head once more. "The child's name," she croaked, "is Fali Enwa."

The village erupted into cheers, and the celebration resumed. Vuli hopped in place next to Montra, excitedly patting his shoulder. "Her name, Montra! It's so wonderful!"

Montra chortled as he grabbed her arms, a futile attempt to try and calm her. "It is wonderful, yes." And he meant that. The Elder Spirits knew all--past, present, future, and they had proven their infinite knowledge to be true time and time again. This was especially true for whenever another Ooawan had been given his or her name. Montra's baby sister, Fali Enwa, was destined for a life of happiness and love. That was what her name meant.

"You are so lucky," Vuli whined as she continued jumping. "I long for a younger sibling to teach, to grow with…" She paused and lowered her voice. "If only my father wasn't still out with the hunting party. He's missing all the fun."

"They'll return soon, aye?"

Vuli offered a shrug, but she looked downcast. "They should have gotten back a day ago."

As if on cue, commotion started from behind them. The lookouts positioned in the trees signaled that somebody was approaching the village. Montra flicked up his ears at the sounds and turned his head to see what was going on. What he saw delighted him at first. Then he realized something was wrong.

"The hunting party has returned!" a male called from within the trees, and Montra's heart fell when he saw them. The party had originally been a team of six. Only two hobbled back into the village now. The lead hunter--Montra thought his name was Ak-tren Sol--walked with a severe limp in his left leg. Blood pooled down his thigh and shin from massive gashes, and he had similar injuries on his torso and arms. The second hunter was missing his right eye. Montra assumed that was due to the raking claw mark on his face. He dragged a leather bag through the snow behind him.

The cheering and laughter stopped, and villagers rushed forward to help. "Father?" Vuli whispered. Montra turned to look at her. Horror consumed her face. She released Montra's arms and sprinted along-side everyone else.

Montra followed after her, and other Ooawans knocked and pushed him aside. He managed to squeeze past a few, but he'd lost Vuli in the crowd. He frantically looked around for her bushy tail, unable to find her.

"Move! Let me through!" he heard his father shout. The crowd shifted a bit as everyone stopped around the scene, and a moment later Montra caught sight of his father hurrying toward the two remaining hunting party members. Aktren collapsed as Father arrived at his side. Father knelt next to Aktren and grasped his shoulders. "Aktren, what happened?"

"The... trees. It was in the trees," Aktren said, although Montra could barely hear him. It was difficult to make out the words over the chattering of the villagers. However, Aktren's voice did sound dry and pained, as if he was struggling to speak, to even stay awake. Montra shoved past more Ooawans not only to find Vuli, but also to better see the injured hunters.

"What of the others?" Montra's father asked as Montra squeezed in between two older Ooawans. Up ahead, he spotted Vuli's tail. She was near the front of the crowd. He hastened to catch up to her.

"It attacked," Aktren continued in his rasp. "We weren't prepared. It stole our food..."

"Aktren," Montra's father said sternly, "what happened to the others?"

There was a long pause as Montra ran. His chest felt tight, his tail twitching with dread. He was racing against what would be said next. Racing to reach Vuli's side before she heard the words he already knew to be true.

Aktren coughed once as the other hunting party member toppled over. "The Rhevan took them," Aktren finally admitted. "It took them all."

Vuli's ears dropped. Montra made it to her side as she let out a scream of anguish. He enveloped her in his arms, and she broke down, crying into his chest.

He looked up, caught sight of his father staring at him. There was concern in Father's eyes, yes, but Montra saw more behind them. There was also resolve, a look that indicated this was the final straw.

A look that indicated it was time to leave, to find a new home.

CHAPTER 3

MONTRA HAD JUST FINISHED PACKING food and water in his bag. He hadn't taken much, only enough for a day. He could make it last at least two if he played things safe. Once he finished handling his provisions, he threw a cloak over his shoulders for warmth and moved on to loading up his spare arrows.

After Father had helped Aktren and the other hunting party member to their respective huts so they could be healed, Montra had set to work gathering and hiding supplies outside of his family's dwelling. His father had come to bed late, but Montra had stayed awake even long after his father returned. Now he was preparing to leave.

He knew that by morning, Father would an-nounce to the village that the time had come to find somewhere else to live. Montra wasn't sad he would be absent for it. If all went well, they wouldn't be leaving at all.

He finished packing his equipment and slung his quiver full of arrows over his shoulder. The bow itself went next. The only items left in his hideout consisted of various things he'd taken from man-camps and -villages. He had collected many artifacts over the years and brought them to this little cove, which was located a short distance down the hill from Nete-Iat Rock. One of the objects was a metal circle of some kind that he had often seen men-females wear on their ears. Such strange behavior…

Among the other items--toys, tools, and pieces of clothing--Montra spotted the most interesting artifact he had ever taken. It was slim, and the protective barrier around it opened to reveal many thin, white, and delicate sheets within. All of the sheets had been decorated with black scratches, and although Montra couldn't be sure what they were exactly, he suspected they contained the word-of-men. In fact, the more he flipped through them, the more he found what he thought were men's writings.

Most curious of all, the front of the object's protective barrier had the image of a man-male and someone else who Montra assumed was the man's young male child. They stood upon a sand-covered area. The larger man was missing a leg, and he held a hefty branch.

Montra had always wondered what the black scratches on the sheets meant when translated to

Ooawan, if they were in fact the word-of-men. Maybe someday he would discover their secrets.

He sighed as he left that last, most fascinating human artifact, and turned to exit the hideout. *I'll only ever know what it is if I manage to make my way back home*, he thought. After all, the hunting party had returned without four of its six members and without the month's worth of food they had been sent away for, and Montra was leaving by himself. He'd be lucky if he was still alive by sunrise.

He stepped out of the cove and tiptoed through the village, careful not to be seen. Since he did this often, he'd become quite stealthy. However, he didn't usually travel so far away.

He passed many huts until he reached the front of the village. It took him a moment to locate the trail Aktren had followed, but once he found it, he--

"Are you leaving?" a female asked, and Montra flinched; he hadn't heard anyone approach. Thankfully, though, he recognized the voice. He swung around to find Vuli sitting against a nearby tree. It seemed to Montra that she had been doing so for some time. She continued, "Are you going away just like everyone else?"

Montra made his way to her side and knelt down next to her. "Vuli, I--"

"I won't stop you," she interrupted. Montra didn't say anything, and she hung her head, wiping her eyes with her palms. "I know why you're leaving. I just wish you didn't have to…"

Montra sighed. Vuli's past was… tragic, to say the least. Ooawans weren't exactly a common sight outside of this village. In fact, Vuli and her father had come here just before the previous winter, and everyone had been surprised about their arrival. They'd come from another village, a community which had been wiped out by sickness. Vuli said she'd watched everyone there die slowly, including her mother. Before she and her father--the last-known survivors of the plague that destroyed their home--had left, their Elder had passed down a sacred talisman to Vuli, the one she wore around her neck.

Montra readjusted the strap of his quiver. "I'm going to kill the thing lurking in these woods."

"The Rhevan," Vuli said.

Shudders slithered down Montra's back. "Aye. If it is no longer hunting our kind, we won't have to leave."

Vuli gave him a curious glance. "Leave?"

"My father told me that if the attacks continued, we would leave the village and find somewhere safer to live. And, well… the attacks are still going on."

Vuli nodded, but the blank expression on her face told Montra she didn't really care. She met his gaze with glistening eyes. "Do you know what the creature is?"

Montra shook his head. "I don't."

"If the others couldn't stop it, then why do you think you can?"

"My father said it can't be fought," he said quietly. "But I have to try. Somebody has to try."

Vuli sat in silence for several moments before climbing to her feet. "Promise me something," she said, a tremor in her words. Montra rose to meet her. "Promise me that you'll do whatever you can to kill it."

Montra opened his mouth to reply, but he couldn't form a response. It surprised him that she hadn't asked to come with him. Not that he would have let her, anyway, but it was still unexpected. He released a long breath. "I promise."

Vuli stepped forward and leaned in close, then pressed her forehead against his. His tail twitched. Her presence was warm, comforting, and the nervousness he usually felt during moments between them was nonexistent. They stood together for what felt like the whole night before Vuli pulled away.

They stared into each other's eyes. "Come back to me," Vuli whispered.

"I will," Montra said, but she didn't seem to believe him. He didn't really believe him, either.

Despite Vuli's obvious doubts, she smiled and patted his chest. "You better. Who else will talk with me about the strange ways of men?"

Montra grinned. "Who else, indeed?" He stepped back. "They'll send a party the moment my father realizes what I've done. Keep them from doing so if you can."

"You feel it, don't you?" she asked. "The storm?"

"Aye." The wind blew gently now. Also, the behavior of the animals around them indicated the weather was changing, and soon. *What a time I've picked to do this.*

"May the Elder Spirits watch over you, Montra Bos," Vuli said.

"And you, Vuli Reywa," he replied, then turned and walked away. With a heavy heart, he relocated the hunting party's trail and began following it farther into the woods.

He trudged along until he arrived at a clearing with two colossal trees standing side by side. This was a landmark he had learned about from his father and brother. They referred to it as Two Trees.

Montra stared at the trees for a while. The hunting party had easily passed between them on the way home, yet Montra couldn't force himself to step forward. It was as if something held him back.

A chill blew through the air, through Montra. He trembled. *What's wrong with me? I have to do this.*

He lowered his tail, his fur bristling, and wrapped the appendage around his legs to keep them warm. Was he just scared? This mission was practically suicide, so being fearful about it made sense. Besides, his kind might be hunters, but they weren't fighters. Pointless violence was not the Ooawan way. So why did he remain intent on walking toward the jaws of a monster? What had drawn him out here?

He produced his dagger and looked down at it. The blade was still slightly loose. Past the weapon, on the ground, blood stained the snow from when Aktren and his companion had returned.

Montra tightened his grip on the knife's handle. His people were dying. His home was being threatened. Maybe Father was fine with packing up and running away, but he wasn't. He had to do this.

He sheathed the dagger and stepped forward. As he passed through the trees, his ears flicked up at a sudden clicking sound. The noise must have come from somewhere nearby. It was faint, as if far away, but that couldn't be…

"*Accept your destiny*," a voice whispered in the wind.

Montra's breath caught in his throat. He spun around and surveyed the brush, but he saw no one. Ears twitching, he tried to detect where the clicking came from, but that was gone now, too. Could he be hearing strange noises due to worry?

The branches overhead rustled. Those could have caused the clicking. Right?

He let out the breath he'd been holding. *I need to stay focused. I'm just hearing things. I have to be.*

Montra turned his focus back on the trail and followed it away from Two Trees.

*E*MBERS FROM THE fire Magnus and Douglas had started crackled softly, floating skyward. The heat the flames provided proved to be a godsend for Magnus's numb limbs.

The pair had hiked a good portion of the day before they'd stopped to set up their tents. Now they sat on logs around the small blaze. "So," Magnus began, "have you ever heard of any cat-creatures like this before?"

Douglas pursed his lips. "Well, there's a few of 'em out there. Mngwa, Weretigers, hell, even the Ozark Howler has some truth behind it. Nothin' like this thing, though."

"Nothing with the ability to make people vanish entirely, you mean," Magnus added.

Douglas held his hands out toward the flames. "Had a buddy tell me a story once, 'bout a monster he hunted in Alaska. Somethin' practically invisible was out killin' folks." He pulled back his hands and rubbed them together. "Turns out there's a legend up there, a legend that talks about a big cat called the 'White Death.' Kills folks, gets a cool stripe down its back for it. Otherwise, an entirely white tiger."

Magnus nodded. "So, a new species of big cat?"

"Almost," Douglas said with a laugh. "My buddy, he killed the thing once he narrowed down how it found its victims. Wasn't invisible, just good at stayin' camouflaged. It also wasn't a solid animal. It was a phantom of some kind."

Magnus furrowed his brow. "A phantom?"

"Not important," Douglas replied, waving a hand. "What I'm sayin' is that new encounters happen pretty often. This cat-creature seems unknown now, but for all we know, it could have been seen throughout history."

Magnus mulled that over without response. He could name a few cases in his time where a seemingly-unknown monster had turned out to have been another more-well-known one. Douglas was right. There was a chance that whatever this thing was, they'd heard about it at some point before. Nothing could hide from humanity for so long... right?

"What about you?" Douglas asked. "Anything fun happen in Twilight Peak lately?"

Magnus shook his head. "Nah. Uneventful as ever."

Douglas chuckled and tucked his hands in his armpits. "Yeah, right. That cursed little slice-of-life is anything but uneventful."

Now it was Magnus's turn to laugh. "Yeah..." He sat for a minute before continuing, "Let's just say Twilight Peak is as unsafe as it's ever been. I'm..." He rubbed his palms together as he stared down at the dancing flames, silently deliberating the best way to say what he was thinking. "I'm just not sure who I can trust anymore."

Douglas let out a low whistle and leaned back on his log. "Things are pretty bad over there, huh?" Magnus nodded again. Things were more than bad, but he couldn't tell Douglas that. Getting anyone involved was risky. Telling anyone too much was a death sentence. "Well," Douglas continued, "if anyone's gonna get things sorted, it's you."

Magnus offered Douglas a smile. "I hope so."

Douglas climbed to his feet and stretched. "Might be time to turn in for the night." He dug around in his pocket and pulled out a weather tracker. "We should probably get up around... Aw, shit."

"What?" Magnus asked, climbing to his feet.

Douglas showed him the device. "There's a blizzard warning in effect now. Storm must'a snuck up on us."

"We should turn back."

Douglas shook his head and stuffed the device back into his coat. "We're closer to the hot zone than we are to Donner Village. I say we wake up early, find the thing and waste it, then get home in time for Christmas."

"We'll be hit by the storm before we find that thing," Magnus argued. "We don't have the gear to survive a blizzard out here."

Douglas shrugged and unzipped his tent. "That's why we'll be on our way back before it gets too bad." With that, he climbed inside and closed the flap.

Magnus stood in the cold for a minute, then got into his tent as well. The fire would keep their campsite warm enough throughout the night, at least until it burned out. And if they were lucky, they wouldn't be dead by this time tomorrow.

Once Magnus sealed the door shut, he wrapped himself up in his thermal sleeping bag and patted his chest. There was a lump missing from inside his coat pocket. *Forgot to put my lighter in my bag*, he thought. It was too late to retrieve it now, though. He was far too comfortable to get back up.

He checked under his pillow for his .44 Magnum. It never hurt to be prepared. With his knife situated close as well, he drifted off into an uneasy sleep, the flames still snapping outside.

CHAPTER 4

THE SOUND OF THE DYING CAMPFIRE was the first thing to catch Magnus's attention as he cracked his eyes open. All he could see, however, was pitch-black. He raised his wrist and checked his watch. *One in the morning... The fire should have died by now.*

He heard another *snap*, and a terrifying realization sobered him out of his half-sleep. That wasn't the sound of a dying fire. That was the sound of branches breaking.

As quickly and quietly as he could, Magnus reached under his pillow and snatched the revolver, then grabbed his knife and slipped out of the sleeping bag. All the while, he listened carefully for more snaps, but soon realized they had ceased. He unzipped the tent flap just enough to peek outside. It was dark, barely illuminated by the moonlight above, the air still and silent, snowflakes still cascading from above. The fire had long since died, most likely an hour or two after they'd gone to bed, which had been four hours ago.

Magnus chanced on unzipping the flap entirely and stepped out into the freezing air. He reached into his shoulder pocket and produced a small flashlight, then held it up and switched it on.

The camp was in disarray. Supply bags they'd left tied to trees had been knocked to the ground in heaps, tracks perforating the snow all around them.

Magnus turned toward Douglas's tent to find Douglas already unzipping his door. He stuck his head out. "What's up?"

Magnus gestured at the junipers and pines surrounding them with his flashlight. "I think something's creeping around camp," he whispered.

Douglas clambered out of the tent with a grunt, rifle in hand, and slapped his cap on his head. "What the hell are we waitin' for, then?"

Together, the pair prowled toward the foliage ahead. Magnus kept his eyes trained on it, watching the branches rustle, the snow fall. His pulse drummed in his ears. He steadied his breathing, trying to stay calm.

A massive shape leapt out from the bushes and rushed forward, away from them. Every nerve in Magnus's body flinched in reflex. He jumped back and caught a flash of brown as the figure darted farther into the forest. He bolted after it, Douglas's feet pounding against the ground behind him.

The figure vaulted over a fallen tree. It was a close call, but Magnus managed to do the same. *I hope Douglas made the jump too. I can't risk looking back now.*

The chase lasted for another minute, but for Magnus's nerves, it felt like eternity. Finally, he followed the figure into a clearing. It stopped, and now he could see it clearly. *You've gotta be kidding me...*

The buck he'd been chasing snorted as it pawed the ground. It lowered its antlers and faced him head-on. He slowly backed away.

Douglas stumbled up next to him. The other man slowed his pace when he spotted the deer. "Aw, hell."

The animal lifted its neck and snorted again. *Don't make me shoot you, please...* It spun around and resumed its run into the woods.

Douglas fixed his cap and slung his rifle over his shoulder. "A deer, Myers? Really?"

"A deer wouldn't have knocked our gear out of the trees," Magnus retorted.

"It was a buck. They rub their antlers on trees, remember?" He checked his watch. "We should head back and pack up anyway. We're running out of time. Storm's movin' in quick." He pivoted and started the walk back.

Just as Magnus was about to follow him, a frightened squeal echoed from the direction the deer had run in. Magnus squinted that way, peering through the pines. *What was that for?*

Douglas huffed from behind Magnus. "Hurry up before I leave your ass here."

Magnus backpedaled several steps, then turned around and jogged after Douglas. "You don't think *that* sounded weird?"

"Of course I do," Douglas replied. "That's why we're headin' back to camp to get our gear."

The snow was falling more intensely by the time they arrived back at camp, and once Magnus saw what the site had been reduced to, his breath caught in his throat.

The tents were shredded as though by animal claws, snow already burying the tattered strips of cloth. Magnus hurried to where his tent had stood mere minutes before and knelt to inspect the damage. All that remained were ragged ribbons of fabric.

"Son of a bitch," Douglas muttered. "We were gone, what? Five, six minutes?"

Magnus glanced around, scanning the area. "Our bags are gone, too."

Douglas slowly turned around. "This thing must've been watchin' us. The second we let our guard down, it swooped in and trashed our tents, stole our stuff, and booked it." He paused, and Magnus faced him. He lowered his rifle and checked the ammunition, then threw it back over his shoulder. "We need to kill that thing now. If we try and go back to town, we'll be hunted, and we'll get stuck between the monster and the storm."

"We didn't even have the means to survive a blizzard in the first place," Magnus yelled. "Going after it now means we can't avoid the storm. We're going to die out here."

Douglas shrugged. "Dead if we do, dead if we don't. At least this way we'll go down savin' lives in the long run." Without another word, he hiked into the trees, in the direction of the shout they'd heard.

Magnus shook his head. *We might die out here. And then what'll happen to our families?* Paige's and Ryan's faces flashed in his mind. What if he never saw them again? *No, no. I can't think like that. I won't die. I'll see Paige and Ryan again. It'll be all right.*

I just have to think of the folks that've gone missing. Remember their faces. Bring them justice.

I can't fail them. I can't fail them like I did Twilight Peak.

With a frustrated sigh, he rose, resigning himself to follow Douglas through the falling snow.

MONTRA SPRINTED THROUGH the foliage with as much stealth as possible. The air grew colder by the moment, the winds increasing in strength. If he didn't hurry, he'd soon lose the trail.

He scanned the ground as he moved, monitoring every sign and track he needed to follow next. Unfortunately, the footprints and scarlet trails had already begun to fade beneath the freshly fallen snow. Despite this, the scent of blood and death remained thick in his nostrils.

It wasn't long before Montra arrived at the remains of what must have been a chaotic scene, and he slid to a stop to investigate. Streaks of red stained the snow.

They even mixed with the white in some spots, creating a dark-pink color. Scraps of brown fur lay scattered around several broken knives and bows. Montra lifted his head to the trees closest to him and saw claw marks. *Where are the bodies?* he wondered.

Surely this was the place where a majority of the hunting party had fallen to the Rhevan. That's what it looked like, anyway. Had the Rhevan taken them away from here?

Montra flicked his ears as he detected a cluster of faraway sounds. Someone or something was releasing a volley of yells, and based on the way they echoed through the trees, Montra guessed whoever or whatever the sounds belonged to were on the move.

He pulled his dagger free and grasped it tight as he dashed forward. He must be getting close now, and if he could catch the Rhevan by surprise, perhaps he could deliver a killing blow.

SCREAMS PIERCED THROUGH the blustering gales, and Magnus took pause to consider where the shrieks could be coming from.

Douglas swung around, his rifle at the ready. He settled on the direction the shouts seemed to be coming from and sprinted that way. "C'mon, let's go!" Magnus huffed and sped after Douglas, revolver in one hand and knife in the other.

More screeches sounded from somewhere up ahead. *Are there others out here besides us?* Magnus couldn't imagine that to be the case. After all, the area was supposed to be locked down. Sure, he and Douglas had snuck in, but who else other than a pair of monster hunters would be crazy enough to do such a thing?

Magnus's heartbeat quickened, and it wasn't only because of all the running they'd been doing. Something told him they were in more danger than they'd initially estimated, if that was even possible. He'd overlooked something obvious, but what?

Douglas jerked to a stop and glanced around. "Where are you?" he yelled into the forest.

Magnus halted behind Douglas and listened intently. Whoever was shrieking sounded close. So close, in fact, that this should be where they were located. Unless something else had reached them first. Or maybe…

Magnus's stomach clenched as realization overcame him. Everything made sense now. *After all my years doing this*, he thought, *I should have known right away.* And it was true. He had been too settled on Douglas's theory of a giant, cat-like monster abducting people that he hadn't stopped to consider the other possibilities.

He seized Douglas by the shoulder. "We need to leave! *Now!*"

"Why?" Douglas asked, irritation lacing his tone. "Don't you hear the yells?"

"Yes, and they aren't coming from people," Magnus replied. "They're coming from whatever it is we're hunting. We had it all wrong!"

Douglas narrowed his eyes. "The hell d'you mean?"

"Think about it. The missing bodies. The area. The time frame. The human voices!"

Douglas considered this before laughing. "You can't be serious."

"I am," Magnus said, checking over Douglas's shoulder for signs of danger.

"You really think it's a Wendigo?" Douglas asked. "You know, they've been hunted out of Donner Pass. Which took a mighty long time, might I add."

Magnus gave Douglas a stern look. "Then one must have slipped through the cracks. Now come on! We need to go!"

"Obviously the creature is agile enough to stay mobile," Douglas continued, seemingly ignoring Magnus's warnings. "And maybe, *maybe* it's smart enough to scream like people do in order to lure us out here. That said, it's more likely that some dumb bastard made the mistake of sneakin' into the woods, just like we did, and got themselves--"

"Shhh!" Magnus interrupted. "Listen."

Douglas paused. Although Magnus figured he'd continue his rant, he stayed silent. For a few moments they stood without speaking, the only sound that of the wind blowing. However, the "peace" didn't bring Magnus solace. If anything, it set off more alarm bells in his head.

"Look, I see what you're sayin'. I do. But we--" A ruby drop landed on Douglas's cap and trickled down to his cheek. His eyes went big, and he pressed his fingers against the fluid and examined them.

Heart pounding, Magnus looked up at the trees, just in time to see something large and brown as it dove toward them.

Magnus jumped back, and Douglas followed his lead. The thing landed with a wet *thonk* in the snow between them, and Magnus soon realized what it was: a headless deer carcass. Blood pooled from the corpse's meaty stump, from where its head had once been. And as Magnus reclaimed his balance, he realized one of the cadaver's front legs had been ripped clean off, most of its stomach torn apart as if it had been eaten through.

Magnus gazed upward once again, his fears confirmed.

A thin, pale figure glared down at them from high above, clinging to the side of the tree next to Magnus. The creature's limbs were long and skeletal, its bald head splattered with fresh blood. Jagged, crooked fangs jutted out from its drool-frothed maw, its virulent eyes a pale shade of gray.

The Wendigo howled, the sound a mixture of a human's scream, a bear's roar, and a deer's call.

"Shit!" Douglas exclaimed. He readied his rifle and fired a round that struck the creature straight in the chest. Its claws came free of the bark, and it crashed to the ground ahead of them. "Come on, Magnus!" Douglas ordered as he turned and ran.

Magnus wasted no time, following Douglas close. Shuffling sounded from behind them. The monster's wicked cry echoed across the sky. Magnus glanced back, caught a flash of gray.

A wet *riiiiip* sounded in the air, and Magnus looked at Douglas. Liquid red sprayed like a water fountain from Douglas's right shoulder, his arm torn from its socket. He tumbled to the ground, bellowing even louder than the Wendigo as he writhed in the snow. His severed limb lay only a few feet away.

Magnus slid to a stop as the Wendigo dropped from above and landed next to Douglas. The man climbed to his knees and stared up at the monster. It lifted its bony arms, wrapped its thin fingers around Douglas's head.

Before Magnus could react, the Wendigo snapped Douglas's neck with a sharp twist. It spun the head around and around, then ripped it clean off. Blood rocketed from the stump.

The Wendigo's eyes settled on Magnus from behind the scarlet shower. *This is it*, he thought. *This is where I die. I love you, Paige. I love you, Ryan. I'm sorry.* He squeezed his tingling fingers around the revolver and the knife he'd been holding so tightly. *Even still, I'm not going down easy.*

Douglas Creed's remains toppled over, and the Wendigo leapt toward Magnus with supernaturally-fast speed, so quick Magnus could barely keep track of the creature.

Magnus hastened backward, keeping his focus on the Wendigo's movements as best he could. It hunched down on all fours, then leapt for him. Magnus fired the revolver. The shot blew into the beast's head, sending its path askew. It crashed into a pine and collapsed.

Magnus knew that even if his gun had bought him a bit of time, his bullets were essentially useless against the monster. However, if he'd gained even a few seconds with that shot, he was grateful.

He slammed back-first into a tree and spun around, stumbling as he tried to get past it. Maintaining his balance, he bounded forward.

Another roar sounded from behind him. The creature must be on its feet again. Magnus pivoted to resume his backward sprint. He raised the revolver and tried to catch sight of the monster.

From up above, the Wendigo hurdled from tree to tree, using them to shield itself. *I can't get a good shot if it's moving like that!*

The monster swung into the open and dove for Magnus. However, just as he fired his gun, he slipped.

The ground beneath him vanished, and he fell down, down, down. The recoil of his shot sent his weapon flying, and his bullet sailed above and beyond the Wendigo's head.

Before he knew it, he was tumbling head over heels down a hill, snow billowing all around him. He tried to reach out, tried to stop himself, but found he could not.

As the minutes passed he rolled farther and faster, and with every flip of his body, he kicked up more white into the wind. Soon it felt as if frost had made its way down his back, beneath his jacket. The Wendigo roared again, but it sounded distant now.

Magnus squeezed his eyes shut as he continued sliding down. Eventually, he struck his head on something hard. Pain arced through his skull, and he fell senseless.

CHAPTER 5

THE SCENT OF BLOOD ASSAULTED MONTRA'S nostrils as he ran, his feet growing more chilled from the ever-growing amount of snow blanketing the forest floor.

A monstrous howl shook the trees, and every hair on Montra's hide stood on end. It sounded like the scream of a man fused with the call of a woodswalker. *Do I really want to get close to this thing?* he thought.

He halted and turned the dagger over in his hand. After a moment's deliberation, he sheathed the weapon and pulled his bow off of his shoulder. He readied an arrow, then continued forward, but he traveled at a slower pace than before.

Soon Montra found himself staring into a clearing, a refuge from the army of frost and lumber. However, after a quick inspection of the area, he realized it was anything but safe.

The smell of gore oozed from a body lying on the ground up ahead. Fluid seeped from the carcass, turning the white powder beneath it a deep shade of red. Little clouds of steam rose from the remains, but they faded almost instantly with the cold and swirling gusts.

A branch snapped. There was a blur of movement above, in the clearing. Montra turned toward the vegetation there. He squinted at the branches, at a second flash of… something, then focused on another tree.

Chills ran down his back. A pale figure clung to the side of the thick timber. It appeared to be a man, but no, it couldn't be. Something was wrong with it. It was much too thin, its arms too long. It even had fangs like an Ooawan's--that is, if Ooawans had an overabundance of teeth in their mouths. *It's the Rhevan*, he thought, swallowing hard.

The Rhevan hopped down from its perch, onto the ground beside the bloodied remains in the clearing, but it happened faster than Montra could process. His kind were excellent at hunting lesser-prey, but now that he could see the way this monster moved… Well, it was no surprise the beast was targeting his village. *They* were the lesser-prey in these woods now.

The Rhevan knelt next to the cadaver, its spoils. It lifted a severed head from the snow, the severed head of a man. The monster inspected the body part for a few moments, then sank its fangs deep into the flesh. The creature whipped its head back and forth and shredded the picking until it was no more than scraps of skin and hair.

Montra looked away, his stomach whirling. He made sure to keep the monster in the corner of his vision, but he could no longer bear witness to this atrocity.

The Rhevan screeched again, a sound so piercing it hurt Montra's ears. He turned back to see the monster as it dropped its meal and held its own head in its hands. The creature appeared to be in a great deal of pain.

Blood burst from its skull. It shrieked, dropping its hands. What Montra watched next was... strange.

Antlers like a woodswalker's sprouted from the Rhevan's head. They grew rapidly in an outward direction. Montra squeezed his bow, the jagged edges of the wood digging into his palm. What *was* this thing? It traveled so fast, and its hunger seemed more than primal. Supposedly, it couldn't be fought, and now it was developing new protuberances?

The screaming continued, and the Rhevan turned sharply in Montra's direction. Its nose and mouth cleaved open, spraying waterfalls of blood onto the ground. Its fangs elongated, its snout enlarging and extending.

When the Rhevan's appearance stopped changing, Montra lowered his weapon. The monster's facial features now looked more like a woodswalker's rather than a man's. Somehow, its build and the shape of its skull had transformed as well, supporting its new attributes. It reared back and released another howl, but this one was even deeper, and somehow more evil, than the others.

Without warning, the creature stabbed its claws into the man's remains, plunged its newly-formed jaws into the severed head, and leapt into the air.

Montra waited a few moments before he rose and gave chase. The Rhevan was leaving with its trophy, so now would be a good time to track the creature to its lair.

That is, if he could keep up with it.

SHARP PAIN REVERBERATED through Magnus's skull as he slowly regained consciousness. He lifted his head, his ears prickling from the glacial temperature, his fingers tingling as he curled them inward.

His body had already been covered with a thin layer of snowfall, and the gales bit at his exposed skin, even more so than before. *How long was I out?*

He climbed to his feet. His legs felt like jelly, but they weren't completely numb. Thankfully, he hadn't been unconscious long enough for the weather to take a firm hold on his body quite yet.

He leaned against a tree, which was possibly the culprit for his headache, considering the way he'd been sitting beside it. As he took in his surroundings, he caught sight of something familiar: the antler-hilt of his knife as it stuck up out of the white powder near his feet.

Magnus snatched up the weapon and held it close. God only knew where his revolver had ended up.

Not like it was gonna do me much good, anyway, he thought. The gun would only serve to buy him time. But his dagger could actually kill the Wendigo, thank goodness.

He sheathed his knife and started the trek up the hill. As he put one trembling foot in front of the other, he tried to recall everything he knew about Wendigo.

Right leg forward. *They're formed when a person resorts to cannibalism to survive.* Left leg forward. *They're better hunters than the men who go after them.* Right leg. *They hibernate for long periods of time before feasting.* Left leg. *They're a strange type of creature, some odd in-between of a monster and a ghost, rendering traditional weapons such as guns and average knives useless.*

Right. *Only two things can kill a Wendigo.* Left. *Fire is the easiest method of disposal.* Right. *The riskier method is a silver blade through the heart.*

He paused for a second, his breaths growing shallow. The most worrying detail of all was the Wendigo's adaptability. The longer it survived, the more it could kill and consume and the more it evolved to fit in with its environment. For whatever period of time the Wendigo was left alive in this world, it would continue to grow faster, to become stronger, to *change*.

And, based on the way the creature had been moving earlier, Magnus guessed it had been around for some time. Most Wendigo had been hunted out of Donner Pass many years ago, but it was possible one of the monsters had been overlooked.

Magnus resumed his climb. A few more minutes passed, and he reached the top of the hill, shivering as he hugged himself tight. His coat had grown soggy from the weather, and after the "nap" he'd had in the snow, the rest of his clothes weren't doing him any favors, either.

He needed to find shelter soon if he wanted to stand a chance in these woods.

*C*LAW MARKS IN the trees led Montra after the Rhevan. He had lost sight of it a while ago, but its faint sounds and scents lingered. Soon, however, its noises had faded entirely, and Montra could only track it by the smell of death it carried and the scratches it made on branches and bark.

Montra slid to a stop to investigate the immediate area. The gouges he had been following had suddenly disappeared. It was as if the creature had vanished into thin air. He flicked up his ears and listened, but all he could hear was the wind. He took a whiff of the surrounding air. The stench of blood and decay grew weaker, fading more with each passing moment.

How could the Rhevan disappear so quickly? he wondered. *No creature can do that. Not man, not Ooawan…*

A sudden realization overcame him. *The wind. I'm losing its scent because I'm following the wind. It must have led me in a circle.*

That means it could have easily picked up my scent.

As if on cue, the sound of powerful claws scraping against bark resumed, only it was much closer than before. Montra spun around and raised his bow.

The Rhevan screeched from its perch high above. Montra loosed an arrow. The projectile struck the monster in the chest... then bounced off without even scratching the creature.

The beast huffed, a stream of mist exiting the bony nostrils of its deformed head. It roared and lunged for Montra.

Montra darted to the side. The Rhevan crashed into the snow. Montra wheeled around and sprinted into the dark. He slung his bow across his back, every muscle in his body tense. He dropped on all fours, ready to run as fast as he could, when the creature sailed overhead. It landed a short distance in front of him.

Montra stopped to change direction, but the Rhevan recovered before he could. The monster advanced for him, fangs bared.

A HORRIFIC WAIL echoed across the forest around Magnus. It was like a shock wave blowing past him.

Must be the Wendigo, he thought. *But it sounds different than before. Sounds close, too.* Wind started pushing against his spine. If the monster intended on finding him, it had probably located him by now. He needed some defense.

There had been times past when, if all he'd had was his knife, he'd have felt just as confident as the instances when he'd been holding a gun. But in these woods, under this storm, against *this* particular monster, he couldn't feel less naked if he'd been stripped of all his garments. Sure, his blade could kill the Wendigo. But how was he supposed to get close enough to use the weapon on the beast without something else to momentarily distract it?

Magnus patted his chest and noticed a lump. *Eureka.* His lighter was still in his interior coat pocket. He searched his surroundings and found a hefty branch sticking out of the snow next to his boots, then unzipped his coat and grabbed at the rest of his attire. His light sweater, the first layer of clothing beneath the camo jackets, was still dry. After his tumble down the hill, it was a miracle everything on him wasn't soaked and freezing.

He tugged on the fabric and heard it tear. He was going to feel the bite of the frost even more now, but at least he had a fighting chance. He raised the bough he'd found and wrapped the newly-ripped strip of sweater tightly around the dryest end. Finally, he took out his metal flip lighter and lit the fabric.

It took a bit for the flames to catch, but after shielding his makeshift torch from the murderous gusts, he managed to wield it properly. The warmth it offered felt heavenly, and the security it brought was a comfort.

Another roar snapped his attention to the left. He turned and held the torch at the ready. Rapid footsteps drew close.

A figure fell through the brush and landed hard in a snowbank up ahead. It writhed around and rolled over. When it noticed Magnus, it halted, and thanks to the golden glow of the fire, he could see it quite clearly.

The being was roughly the size and shape of a teenage boy, so Magnus assumed it was a "he." Brown fur covered his head and body--at least, what Magnus could see of those things, anyway. A cloak crafted from hides hid the rest of his figure. Pointed ears topped his head, while his bright-yellow eyes--the eyes of a cat--stared up at Magnus with vigilance. The creature cradled his injured left arm, blood leaking from his wounds.

They stared at one another for what felt like years. Magnus couldn't think. Couldn't speak. He had been right; the culprit of the missing people *was* a Wendigo. There were no doubts about that. Douglas, on the other hand, had also been correct. That mysterious cat-creature was--

The being's ears turned. His eyes grew big. He dove sideways as the Wendigo came barreling through the icy air. The monster's claws raked across the cat-creature's right shoulder, barely missing him.

The Wendigo must have seen Magnus. It turned its newly-formed head toward him and opened its blood-covered jaws wide, emitting an earsplitting shriek.

Magnus rushed forward before the monster had the chance to move. He brandished his torch at it. It shrieked and backed away. Magnus pressed on, swinging again. The beast reared up on its hind legs, the flames singing its skin. It yelped in pain and leapt into the trees.

Magnus pivoted in time to see the cat-creature flee farther into the woods. He took off with the closest thing to a sprint he could manage, following the cat, his torch held high. He glanced over his shoulder a few times to ensure the Wendigo wasn't following them.

Soon the cat-creature vanished. And once Magnus took a couple more lunges, he realized why.

Again the ground betrayed him, and he tumbled into pitch-black. Whole minutes passed before he landed hard on a rocky slope, the oxygen escaping his lungs upon impact. His torch slipped from his hand and skidded down the incline. He tried to scramble after it. It slid off another ledge.

Magnus followed the torch, clambering over the lip. There was a short drop, and then he landed on his ribs.

The already-weak flames of his weapon and light source faded. The last thing he saw before the fire died was the wary face of the cat-creature sprawled across the cave floor up ahead.

The last thing he heard before darkness claimed the both of them, however, was the distant yowl of the Wendigo, and the whistling of the unforgiving winter gales above.

CHAPTER 6

THE WALL OF THE CAVE MAGNUS RESTED against was cool, but it was still leagues warmer than outside. It had taken him a few minutes to regulate his breathing after his run and fall, and he'd spent that time listening. Thankfully, the calls of the evil hunting him had since dwindled.

The more recurring sound was that of the constant shuffling of his new companion. Whatever the cat was doing, he sounded frustrated.

Magnus reached into his pocket and produced his lighter, then snapped it open and switched it on. The flame offered a dim but necessary glow, and Magnus looked at the creature sitting across from him. The cat stared at the lighter intently, as if caught off guard by the sudden illumination.

Magnus held up the tool to further inspect the being and caught sight of his mangled arm. He had done a sloppy job of half-tying scarlet-stained wrappings around his wounds. Now that Magnus was closer and had a decent amount of light, he could see how deep the lacerations were. He cautiously scooted forward. "Need some help with that?"

The cat remained quiet, his eyes full of an intelligence that held Magnus's attention. It was as though the creature were having an entire conversation with him that he wasn't privy to. *I've never seen anything like him before*, Magnus thought. Still, the being didn't answer his question, so Magnus reached toward him.

He jerked away. "Reve-stal en corpa nam!"

Magnus leaned back and raised a hand in defense. "Whoa, all right. It's okay."

The creature eased slightly and watched Magnus as he continued wrapping his arm. He tried securing it with his free hand and winced.

Magnus reached for him again. He whipped out a dagger and pointed the blade at Magnus's chest. Magnus kept his unoccupied palm up and open. "It's okay, fella. I'm just trying to help you." He pointed at the bandages. "I can help you do that. Help make ya feel better."

They stared at one another for a few seconds before the cat lowered his dagger. Magnus took that as a positive sign, inching closer. He pointed at the lighter in his hand before handing it over. "Can you hold this?" The cat furrowed his brow. He clearly didn't know what Magnus was asking.

Magnus reached for the creature's injured arm. The being lifted his dagger and pressed the tip of the blade against Magnus's coat. Magnus made his next movements as slow and cautious as possible, gently opening the fingers of the creature's free hand. He set the lighter in the cat's humanoid palm and closed the furry fingers around the object, then lifted his index and pointed at his own eyeballs. "I can't see in the dark." The being sat for a while before lowering his knife again.

Taking this as permission to work, Magnus readjusted the wound's bindings. He not only tightened the fabric, but he also wrapped another clean strip around the cat's arm. The bandages would need to be changed within the next few hours, but they would hold for now.

Once Magnus finished the job, he took back the lighter and gave the creature some room. The cat lifted his arm and moved it around a bit, then turned toward Magnus. "Kindre."

Magnus smiled. He didn't understand whatever it was the being had said, but he guessed it was a form of thanks. He pressed a palm to his chest. "Magnus."

The cat tilted his head to one side. "M-Magnus?"

Magnus nodded happily. "Magnus." He gestured toward the creature.

The being paused before readjusting his posture and mimicking Magnus's actions. "Montra Bos."

Montra Boss? Magnus thought. He wasn't sure if he'd heard that correctly. *Maybe I should stick with Boss for now. I'm probably gonna have a hard time remembering his full name and how to say it properly, at least while we're fighting for our lives.*

Magnus scooted back and rested against the wall on his side of the cave, then raised the lighter and gave their surroundings a better look. Despite the lack of proper illumination, he could see just how tiny this cavity in the earth was. It had enough room for them to stand, but only barely. Magnus gazed to the left, where the cave continued. Darkness beckoned him, but it seemed that the walls expanded the farther the cavern went. They weren't trapped in a dead-end just yet.

Magnus's gut growled. *Ah, dammit*, he thought. It had been some time since he'd last eaten, and his provisions were gone. He rested a hand on his stomach as he shifted onto his other side and glanced up to where he and Boss had fallen in from. It didn't seem easy to climb.

"Magnus," Boss said.

Magnus turned to see that Boss was offering him a handful of berries. He accepted the offer graciously and, after inspecting the berries, decided they were safe to eat. He tossed a couple into his mouth and chewed, their sweet flavor dancing on his tongue. *When was the last time I ate? God, it must have been when I was sitting around the campfire with Douglas.*

The other man's name resurrected gruesome images in Magnus's thoughts. His horrified expression as the Wendigo ripped his head from his body. The geyser of blood erupting from the stump. What was left of his body falling into the snow.

Douglas Creed had not been a perfect man, but he had been a fellow hunter and an old friend. He deserved a proper burial, not to become another pile of bones sitting in the Wendigo's lair.

"Se Rhevan," Boss said. Magnus pushed away the memories of his fallen companion and refocused on his new one. "Tu kes felt arma?" Boss continued. It sounded like a question.

Magnus stared dumbly at Boss. He wasn't sure how to respond. "What?"

"Se Rhevan," Boss repeated, jerking his head upward. *Does he mean the Wendigo?* Boss slashed his dagger through the air once, twice. "Tu kes delt fi morta, felt arma, jusen-fur?"

Magnus shrugged. "I don't understand."

Boss sighed in frustration. He pointed at the opening in the cave and repeated the gashing motion.

Magnus tilted his head. *Is he asking me if we can kill it?* He bent over and examined the ground, finding a decently-sized stone, and climbed to his feet. He dragged the rock across the wall, carving into it until he'd finished his drawing. It was a crude image of the evil hunting them, but he hoped it would help him and Boss understand each other.

He turned around, and Boss nodded. "Se Rhevan." The cat-creature rose to his feet alongside Magnus and pointed his knife at the sketch. Magnus cupped his hand over Boss's and had him lower the weapon. When he looked up at Magnus again, Magnus shook his head.

For a few moments, Magnus examined Boss's dagger. The handle had been crafted from bone, the blade formed from a sharpened stone in the shape of an arrowhead. The two pieces had been tied together with strings and straps fashioned from animal hides. The memory of Douglas laughing at the absurdity of monsters making their own tools popped up in Magnus's mind, and he couldn't help but smile a little.

He turned his attention to Boss and pointed at the knife. "This *won't* kill." He shook his head in an attempt to communicate his point.

Boss narrowed his eyes. "Kill?"

Magnus turned toward the drawing and made stabbing motions at its chest. "Kill."

Montra nodded. He seemed to understand. "*Kill.*" His ears perked up. He snatched his bow and pulled the drawstring back, pretending to ready an arrow. "Kill?"

Magnus shook his head, and the creature's ears drooped. He lowered his bow, a puzzled expression on his face. Magnus raised the lighter to the picture. When Boss looked at him, he tapped the object against the wall and nodded. "Kill." At this, Boss's ears perked up again.

Magnus drew his own knife, the one with the pure-silver blade, and held it up for Boss to see. Once the cat-creature had gotten a good look, Magnus pressed the tip against the drawing's chest. "Kill."

Boss's tail swung back and forth. He huffed, seemingly doubtful. "Se Rhevan del fahsk," he mumbled.

Magnus spied the arrows in Boss's quiver, which lay on the ground nearby. *We might just get out of this yet.*

For the next fifteen minutes, Magnus and Boss deconstructed the arrows, and Magnus returned the arrowheads to Boss before he lumped the branches together.

Using the bindings that once held heads to shafts, Magnus tied the sticks together, then wrapped the remaining materials at the top and started them on fire with his lighter.

The newly-formed torch illuminated the path ahead. And once Magnus and Boss had gathered all their gear, Magnus led the way forward.

He rounded the corner on the right and saw that this tunnel not only grew more spacious, but that it continued on far ahead of them. *It's like some kind of underground system*, he thought. *Maybe that's how the Wendigo moves between the ski resort and Donner Village.*

As they walked, he toyed around with the idea. Every once in a while, he glanced over his shoulder to ensure Boss was safe behind him. The cat-creature seemed wary, but he followed close.

Magnus took deep breaths, trying to remain calm as they trekked into what felt like the belly of the beast.

WINTER WIND SHOOK Atwa out of his deep slumber. He rolled over to see Sel fast asleep beside him. Their newborn, Fali Enwa, rested between them. The baby squirmed uncomfortably, and Atwa guessed she was cold.

He tucked the child's covers over her tiny body, climbed to his feet, and stretched his limbs. His whiskers twitched, and he pivoted, finding Montra's bed empty. He sighed and curled his tail. *Seems he's wandered off again*, he thought.

Atwa wasted no time in retrieving his dagger and securing the strap of its sheath over his shoulder. He tore open the flaps of his family's hut and stepped outside, into the crisp air.

Even through his thick coat of fur, the gusts chilled him. The weather was getting bad, and he knew better than anyone just how frigid it would become. Winter was already the harshest of seasons, and it would only grow worse as the days passed. Finding a new home could be risky in the snow, but waiting for warmer weather wasn't an option. The village didn't have enough food to last even two or three more moons, let alone the entire winter.

Atwa headed for the edge of the village, in the direction of Two Trees. It was a trip he made regularly, considering Montra had made a habit of wandering down the mountain.

"Montra is gone," a female's voice called after him. Atwa swung around to see Sina Weltoo, the Village Elder. She sat atop a boulder surrounded by many other huts.

Atwa stepped toward her. "Sina, it's too cold for you out here. You must return to your hut before you catch your death."

Sina smiled, her empty, pale-gray eyes staring forward. "Eventually, death comes for us all, Atwa."

Atwa climbed onto the boulder and rested a hand on her shoulder. "Let me walk you to a warmer place, then."

One of Sina's hairless hands shot up and clutched Atwa's wrist tightly. "I shall die in warmth. Let me enjoy the cold while I can."

Atwa paused. Her strength and words caught him off guard. It wasn't abnormal for her to utter strange things. She was in tune with the Elder Spirits, after all. It wasn't common for her to be so persistent, though. He sighed. "As you wish."

Sina loosened her grip but didn't let go. "You mustn't follow him."

"What?" Atwa remembered what she'd said moments before. "Wait, what did you mean when you said Montra is gone? How do you know he is missing?"

Sina turned to face him, though her eyes were still blank. "He left hours ago."

Atwa looked to the sky, watching the snow fall around him. *That cub is going to get himself killed.* How many times had he told Montra to stay in the village? How many more instances would he need to? "Where did he go, Sina?"

"Into the woods."

Atwa waited for her to say more, but she remained quiet. Finally, he gave her a gentle pat on the back. "Then I will go and find him." He stood, jumped off the boulder, and began walking away.

"There's no point," Sina replied, her voice calm. "Montra is already dead."

Atwa froze. He swiveled around and examined her features. *She's wrong. Montra can't be...*

Sina's lips curled in a smile. "The cub you once knew him to be is dead, anyway. The Ooawan in those woods is no longer your son." She lifted her head toward the sky. "He's become someone greater than you and I."

Sina's words didn't make sense. Atwa knew how often she spoke in riddles, how often she hinted at events yet to come. Normally, he would cast his doubts aside and place his faith in those who watched over the village. But this was different. This time he couldn't do that. This time, his son was lost in the forest with an unkillable evil.

His breath hovered in a thick mist in front of him before dissipating in the wind. He opened his mouth to speak, but found he was unsure of what to say.

Sina held her grin as she stared vacantly at the sky. Despite everything threatening their survival, she seemed peaceful.

Atwa focused back on the trees. *Montra... what have you done?*

CHAPTER 7

MONTRA FOLLOWED MAGNUS CLOSELY AS they continued marching through the dark. It hadn't been long since they'd wandered beyond their starting point, and Magnus used his makeshift torch to light their way. Montra guessed men couldn't see in the dark as well as Ooawans could.

Montra wasn't exactly sure what he thought of the man yet, either. He had witnessed many strange behaviors exhibited by Magnus's kind, but something about Magnus was different from the rest. He was strong yet gentle. He was friendly yet authoritative. All of that put Montra at ease. In fact, Montra had already begun to think Magnus could be similar to his father in more ways than one.

Montra should have been more on guard, should have been more protective of his well-being around a complete stranger, around a *man*. But for whatever reason, he felt comfortable around Magnus.

Not only that, but because of Magnus, Montra understood the fact that neither of his weapons could have slain the Rhevan, and he was comforted knowing he wouldn't have to battle this evil alone any longer.

A familiar, sickening scent found its way into Montra's nose. "Magnus," he whispered. When the man turned, Montra tapped his own bloodstained arm and pointed at his nose, sniffing audibly. "Blood."

Magnus stood for a moment, processing what Montra had said, then nodded and carefully treaded forward.

Soon they approached another corner, the smell of death and decay growing stronger as they approached it. Montra covered his nose with his forearm as they rounded the junction, traveling to the right, and stepped into another area, this one much larger and more open than the ones they'd previously traversed. However, while the rest of the chambers had been empty, this one was not.

And what waited for them here made Montra's stomach sick.

The cavern was filled with corpses. Some were human, some Ooawan, some woodswalkers and other lesser-prey found in the area. Many were heaped in piles, while others were strung up, dangling from the arched ceiling like macabre hut decorations. Blood pooled out from beneath the bodies, and as Magnus led Montra forward, Montra found it difficult not to make contact with the scarlet liquid. *This must be the creature's den*, he thought, shivering.

Magnus paused as they reached the remains of an Ooawan. To Montra's surprise, Magnus looked down at the male with a sorrowful expression. The Ooawan's head was missing, but based on his stripes and fur color, Montra knew him to be one of the hunting party members who had been lost. Some of the figures around his remains were even more foul, though. Several smelled and appeared to be weeks old.

Magnus stepped over outstretched limbs, and Montra tore his gaze away from the cadaver of one of his own to follow his new companion.

A few more moments passed, and Magnus offered the torch to Montra. Montra accepted, and Magnus knelt down next to another one of the corpses. This one was a man. Magnus undid the bag that was strapped to the man's back and began searching through its contents. A few moments passed before Magnus pulled out three orange dagger-handle-sized objects that had been strapped together with a thin yellow strip.

Magnus let out a long exhale of relief and clutched the objects to his chest. Montra wasn't sure what the man needed them for, but he supposed they must be lucky finds for the situation he and Magnus had found themselves in.

Magnus turned back to Montra and held up the orange things. "Kill," he said, his tone far more reassuring than before, and Montra cocked his head. If he'd understood Magnus correctly, then somehow these objects could kill the Rhevan.

"If you say so," he muttered. He knew Magnus didn't understand his words. But based on the way Magnus chuckled and shook his head, Montra guessed the man sensed his disbelief.

Magnus stood and took back the torch, and together they examined their surroundings more closely. It didn't take long for Magnus to point out another opening ahead of them.

As the pair maneuvered around the rest of the bodies, Montra's whiskers began twitching. His senses ran on high alert, the fur on his tail standing on end. Something was very, very wrong.

There was a flash of movement in the corner of Montra's vision. He glanced around, trying to spot the culprit, but found nothing. Heart racing, he grabbed Magnus by the shoulder. "Something's wrong."

Magnus halted, and when the man turned to meet Montra's eyes, Montra curled his tail to show his fear. Understanding came over Magnus's expression, and he seized Montra's arm and pushed on ahead.

They moved as quickly as they could manage over the lake of carcasses. Finally, they arrived at the next opening in the cavern. They hurried through, into a new area, finding it just as spacious as the last but with a steep ledge off to the right.

The howl of the Rhevan echoed from behind them. Montra spun around, saw the monster leap down from the ceiling. It landed beside him.

Magnus brandished the torch. The Rhevan ducked beneath the attack. Montra reached for his dagger, but the beast swung a thin arm at them, swatting them backward. Montra stumbled and fell. He landed hard on his spine, slid toward the chamber's cliffside.

Montra tried to cry out as he sailed over the edge, into complete darkness, but the wind had been knocked out of him. It was only moments before he crash-landed against another hard surface, his wounded arm aching at the impact. *Magnus*, he thought, gasping for breath, trying to scramble to his feet so he could climb back up. *I must get back to him before it's too late. He needs my help!*

He cannot defeat the Rhevan alone!

*M*AGNUS SLAMMED INTO the cave floor. He recovered quickly, rolling onto his hands and knees. The glow of the torch ahead caught his eye. It slid to a stop, just out of reach.

The Wendigo chittered, rising up on its hind legs. Its head spasmed as it looked around, and finally its attention fell on Magnus. He snatched the pack of emergency flares he'd found in the last chamber and ripped one free. The other two dropped to the ground, but he couldn't focus on that right now.

Without error, Magnus pulled the cap off of the flare and dragged it across the top. Just as the monster lunged forward, the tool ignited. It *crack, crack, crack*-led, bathing the cave with a brilliant red gleam.

The Wendigo screeched and backed away. Magnus chanced a brief glimpse at the ledge but kept his attention on the monster. "Boss? Are you okay?"

No answer. Magnus sighed and drew his pure-silver knife. *This isn't good*, he thought. Sure, he had the flares, but those were only a temporary distraction unless he could jab the beast with them. Even with his blade, the odds of him taking down a Wendigo one-on-one were slim.

The creature seemed to sense his rising panic. It roared and advanced for him. Magnus raised the flare, but the monster veered to the left. Magnus ducked to the right, but he wasn't fast enough. The tips of the beast's claws raked across his back.

He dropped the flare and stumbled backward, pain erupting from his wounds, through his body. He slashed his knife at the Wendigo. The blade tore through the air, scratched an antler tip. Unaffected by the blow, the creature lunged forward. Its horns stabbed him in the stomach and hip, just barely piercing through his thick clothing and his skin. The beast flung him sideways.

Magnus rammed into the ground, on his injured back. Pain seared through him, the knife slipping from his hand. He grabbed at it, but it skidded away until it disappeared over the ledge just as Boss had.

The other flares, he thought. *Gotta get those or I'm done for.* He struggled to his hands and knees, hot agony arcing through his body, and began the crawl toward the remaining flares.

Something sharp speared his leg just above the ankle. He looked back, saw the Wendigo as it bit down hard and whipped its head upward. It pitched Magnus over its shoulder. Stomach clenching, he crashed into the closest wall and crumpled to the cave floor.

Torturous throbs drummed in his back and chest. He tried to keep his eyes agape, but they forced themselves shut. When he managed to open them again, he saw the beast standing over him. It licked its maw clean with a long, pale tongue. Pinkish drool dribbled from its lipless fangs, oozing onto Magnus's face and throat.

It knelt close, almost brushed Magnus's nose with what it had left of its own. The smell coming off of it was putrid, the scent of murder and rot, a magnified odor of what lay in the cavern behind them.

The Wendigo growled and unhinged its jaw, and all Magnus could think was that he'd never see his daughter and grandson again.

Before the monster could finish him off, a silver blade pierced its chest.

The Wendigo released a pained yell. It stood up, a white glow blazing from its chest. *My knife*, Magnus thought. *Boss must've gotten my knife. He's all right.*

There was no other explanation. The pure-silver blade had revealed the creature's heart. A bright, ice-blue outline of the organ beat steadily within its chest. However, Magnus could see the dagger was a finger's length too far from killing the creature.

Boss clung to the Wendigo's back with one hand, grasping the knife's handle with the other. The beast thrashed and flailed. Boss lost his hold and toppled to the ground spine-first, but sprang back to his feet in an instant.

Magnus pointed to the left. "Get the flares!" Boss followed the direction of Magnus's finger with incredible speed and scooped them up.

The Wendigo reached back, trying to remove the dagger lodged between its shoulder blades. It clenched its fingers around the handle and yanked the blade free, then tossed the weapon aside.

Boss gave Magnus a panicked look. He still held the flares. Magnus mimed the action of lighting a flare. Boss lifted one and stared at its cap.

The Wendigo pounced toward Boss, but he somersaulted beneath the attack and dashed to the side. The monster hacked its claws through the air and caught Boss's cloak. Boss staggered back, the flares flying from his grip, and the creature jerked him toward itself. However, he used his pelt as leverage, latching onto it and bounding up toward the Wendigo. He swung behind it, wrapping the hide around the beast's head and blocking its sight.

It chomped through the cloak with ease and whipped Boss away. *I gotta help him*, Magnus thought. He lifted his head, looked around, and spotted the first flare a few feet to the right, its red flames still shining bright. Sucking in a sharp breath and bracing himself for the pain to come, Magnus began crawling toward it.

81

In his peripheral vision, he could see Boss as the cat dove for the flares he'd dropped, but the Wendigo snatched him by the neck and lifted him up toward its face, unhinging its jaw. Boss drew his dagger and stabbed it straight into one of the beast's eyes. There was a loud *snap*, and the monster shrieked. Boss tumbled from its grasp.

Boss landed hard, his knife now broken. The Wendigo tottered backward, clutching its face.

With what felt like the last of his strength, Magnus neared the lit flare and reached for it. However, only the tips of his fingers brushed against the object. He poked it, turning it slightly, then seized it and rolled onto his side. "Boss!"

When Boss looked over, Magnus tossed the flare, sending it soaring. Boss swooped in to catch it, but the Wendigo intercepted him. It readied its mouth to feed, but Boss stuffed his dagger-handle between its teeth. It bit down. The bones of the handle cracked under its bite, but they didn't break. The flare landed on the cave floor beside Boss and the Wendigo.

Magnus scrambled toward the brawl as fast as he could, tried to get there in time to help, but his vision was fading between red and black. He wasn't sure how much longer he could hold on.

The Wendigo bit down once more, but still the bones held strong. Boss glanced at the flare. He stretched out his tail as if reaching for it.

Just as Boss succeeded in wrapping his tail around the flare's shaft, the monster grabbed him by the throat and lifted him into the air. The bones from Boss's weapon finally snapped and fell to the ground. The beast opened its mouth wide.

Just as the Wendigo was about to feast, Boss snatched the flare from his tail and plunged the tip into the monster's chest.

It screamed, ruby flames exploding from the point of impact, already burning the creature's flesh away. Magnus watched as its ice-blue heart thumped four more times before the organ was consumed by fire.

The beast released Boss and lurched to the side. Its arm broke off at the shoulder and fell to the ground. Its mandible followed suit, then its antlers, then its legs.

The Wendigo crumpled to the cave floor in a heap, its screech waning to no more than a croaking whisper as the inferno absorbed its body and turned it to ash.

Relief flooded Magnus's senses, and he stopped crawling toward Boss, his whole body aching. He'd thought once the evil was slain, he would be happy. He'd thought he would cheer and clap, but now that it was dead, he found he could only sigh, close his eyes, and lay down. It was over. Finally over.

When he found the strength to look up again, he saw Boss standing over the Wendigo's ashes. Embers flickered above a few last miniature flames. The cat dropped the flare onto what remained, his ears drooping.

Magnus grunted as he climbed to his feet. His leg was too wounded to put much pressure on it, so he had to limp over to Boss. The pain in his hip and stomach made the movement even more difficult, but it was nothing compared to some of the injuries he'd obtained in the past.

He rested a hand on Boss's furry shoulder. The cat-creature looked at Magnus and smiled. Tears gathered in the edges of his bright-yellow eyes, and he turned back toward the deceased monster.

At that moment, no words were shared between them, but Magnus felt as if they possessed a deep understanding of one another. After all, he had seen what lay in the cavern before this one. The Wendigo had not only hunted and killed men, but Boss's kind, too. Its wrath had plagued them both.

For some reason, it seemed fitting that they had come together to destroy it.

Magnus gasped as more pain tore through his body. He lowered himself to the ground. Boss retrieved his cloak and handed it to Magnus.

Despite his injuries, Magnus smiled and accepted the offering. Together, they tore off strips of it and wrapped Magnus's wounds as best as they could.

After a few minutes of rest, Magnus climbed to his feet and collected the remaining flares. His makeshift torch had begun to die, and the flare Boss had used to slay the monster had also been spent. He would have preferred to sit longer, but their light was fading, and they needed to leave.

Boss aided Magnus as they journeyed out of the cave. Together, they'd find their way back to the surface.

EPILOGUE

*E*ARLY MORNING SUN PEEKED OVER THE horizon, bathing the sky with brilliant orange light. The last of the snow had already fallen, and the white powder *crunch*ed beneath Magnus's boots as he and Boss struggled through the woods.

Pain jolted up and down Magnus's leg as they traveled. Quite frankly, his whole body hurt, and he couldn't catch his breath. More than anything, he wanted to sit and rest. The pair had been traversing the forest for hours since they had escaped the cave system, and every time Magnus motioned that he wanted to stop, Boss would pull him along and say, "Se Ishtan fur helt."

Magnus closed his eyes and continued limping alongside the cat-creature, tingles rallying in his limbs. There was no protection from the cold anymore.

After another hour of walking, Magnus heard voices ahead of them. Had Boss taken him to Donner Village?

He opened his eyes and lifted his head. More cats--more of Boss's kind--with varying fur colors and patterns, had gathered farther up the path, up the hill. Huts stood behind the creatures, a bonfire burning in the center of it all. *No*, Magnus thought. *He didn't take me to Donner Village. He took me to* his *village.*

One of the cats made his way to the front of the crowd. He was tall, with dark-brown fur and white stripes, a dagger hanging at his waist. He shoved past the others, froze when he spotted Magnus and Boss. "Montra!" He hurried down the mound and stopped before them, giving Magnus a wary look before turning his attention to Boss. "Welt fortra se Man?"

"Se Man calsit felt morta se Rhevan," Boss replied.

The other cat turned toward Magnus, his eyes wide. "En se Man calsit sil."

Magnus patted Boss on the back, swaying to the side as he tried to keep his balance. Boss led him to the stump of a tree nearby and helped him sit, then turned back to the other cat. The new creature took a tentative step toward Magnus. He paused, glanced at Boss, then faced Magnus and spoke. "You... help Montra?"

Magnus opened his mouth to respond, but all words escaped him. This one could speak English? Magnus turned toward Boss, and Boss appeared to be just as shocked as he was. He faced the cat who could speak English and nodded. "Montra, he helped *me*."

The English-speaking cat let out a long breath and stared at the ground. He flicked his tail back and forth a few times. When he finally looked at Magnus again, his tail went still. He knelt down so that he was eye level with the man. "We help, too. Heal you. Take you back."

Magnus exhaled in relief. "Thank you."

The English-speaking cat stood and turned his attention to the crowd. "Ashten calist se Man!" At his call, three more creatures scampered down the hill, quickly arriving at Magnus's side. They helped him to his feet, then lifted him up into their arms and carried him toward the village.

Magnus closed his eyes, warm solace settling in his body. He wasn't sure why, but it felt as if he were entering a new world. He allowed his worries to be washed away, all unease disintegrating, and drifted off into a deep and restful slumber.

*M*ONTRA WATCHED AS Magnus was carried away, his muscles stiff and sore as he slumped down onto the stump the man had just been resting on. Between the beating he had taken from the Rhevan and helping Magnus all the way to the village, he was on the verge of falling asleep where he sat.

His father pivoted to glare at him. "What you did was foolish, reckless, and suicidal."

Montra lowered his ears. "Yes."

"What possessed you to go after the Rhevan?" His father knelt next to him. "You've come home injured, and you brought a man. The cold could have killed you if the monster hadn't. Why did you risk your life to fight it in the first place?"

Montra stared hard at his father. "Someone had to take that risk. This is our home. *My* home."

The elder Ooawan said nothing for a few moments. Eventually, he rested a hand on Montra's shoulder and squeezed. "I'm just grateful you're still alive, my son."

Now it was Montra's turn to be silent. A shout sounded from up the hill, and when Montra and Atwa glanced that way, Montra saw Vuli hurrying toward them. Natwa and Mother approached them as well.

Father gave him one last stern look. "We'll discuss this later. I must organize materials and space to accommodate the man."

The Village Leader rose to leave. As he began walking away, Montra said, "Magnus."

He swung around. "Hmmm?"

"The man," Montra said. "His name is Magnus."

Father's whiskers twitched before he trudged off. He paused to talk with Montra's mother, but Natwa and Vuli shot past them, rushing to Montra's side.

Vuli slammed into Montra, nearly knocking him off the stump before hugging him so tightly he thought she might squeeze the breath from his body. "You came back!" she exclaimed.

Montra readjusted and returned her squeeze. "I promised you I would, didn't I?"

"You gave all of us quite the scare, Brother," Natwa said, and Montra could tell by the tone in his voice he was relieved. "We thought the Rhevan would claim you as well."

"I did, too," Montra admitted. "But the woods are safe for us once more."

Vuli released him. "It has been slain?"

He smiled at her. "Yes. It won't be hunting our kind any longer."

Vuli smiled back and enveloped him in another embrace. She rubbed her cheek against his and whispered, "Thank you."

Montra held her as they sat together, and Natwa patted Montra's shoulder. "What was it?" Natwa asked. "The Rhevan, I mean."

At this question, memories of the monster resurrected in Montra's mind. He recalled the way it had transformed its appearance in the woods. Its primal hunger. How quickly it had moved from place to place. The wicked sounds it emitted. "The Rhevan was pure evil," he answered.

However, now was not the time to think of monsters. Now was the time to be thankful for his return home beneath the morning sun.

To be thankful that the nightmare was over.

*M*AGNUS HIKED THROUGH the trees alongside Boss and Boss's father, who Magnus had learned was named Atwa.

The cold hadn't relented since he and Boss had first reached the Ooawan village two days ago, but the forest itself felt much livelier. After he'd dozed off following their arrival, he'd slept the rest of the day. However, he'd woken later in the night, which was when he'd shared a hearty meal with Boss, Atwa, and the rest of their family.

Magnus had rested the next day, but he had also spent time among the Ooawans, picking up whatever bits and pieces he could of their culture. Not only that, but Atwa had explained to Magnus how he knew English. Apparently, the knowledge of human languages had been passed down for generations to Elders and Village Leaders for when the Ooawans might need to communicate with men.

Today was Magnus's third day in the company of Boss and Atwa, and although he had just begun to stand on his injured leg, he'd managed to walk on it decently enough that he'd felt up for the journey home.

The trek had taken hours, but in the end they'd found familiar terrain. Once Magnus realized he'd seen the surrounding trees during his first day in the woods with Douglas, Atwa and Boss had stopped. It was time to say their farewells.

Atwa pointed through the brush ahead. "Man-village not far. You continue alone."

Magnus tentatively stepped forward. Donner Village was still a ways away, but he could make out the road where he and Douglas had left their vehicles. After that, it wasn't much farther. "Thank you," Magnus said, and turned back to the Ooawans. "For everything."

Atwa flicked his tail. "You save Montra. Kill Rhevan. Help my home. Thank *you*."

Magnus smiled and faced Boss. "You take care of yourself, young one. No more running into the forest after monsters."

Atwa laughed and elbowed Boss. "Magnus het del galte fenshir ishtian se fors."

Boss offered a guilty smile. "Kel disn't. Sol de cor fins estart."

"He say he will not," Atwa translated for Magnus. "Also say to visit again, someday."

Magnus chuckled. "I just might."

Atwa appeared unsure of that, but he smiled anyway. "Goodbye, Magnus."

"Goodbye," Magnus replied as Atwa and Boss turned around to begin the voyage back. He watched them walk for a few seconds, a question that had plagued him for most of his stay in their village resurfacing. "Atwa?" he called. The Ooawans halted to face him. He put his hands in his coat pockets. "I understand wanting to keep your home and family safe. I'll keep your secret; you have my word. But why let me go? You could have easily killed me."

Atwa seemed to mull this over, studying Magnus with his bright-yellow eyes. "Senseless killing not Ooawan way." Magnus didn't reply. Nothing else needed to be said.

Atwa and Boss seemed to feel the same, and they left without another word. Magnus did so as well, heading in the direction of Donner Village. His injuries were killing him, but he'd dealt with worse before. Bodily trauma was simply part of the job.

Someday, he knew he would return to the Ooawan village, and maybe he could help them the way they had helped him. In the short time he'd spent with them, they had even told him stories--including the one he'd been tangled up in, which had been Boss's hopeless mission to kill the Wendigo. Apparently, no one had sent Boss to do it. He'd simply taken it upon himself. The kid had put his life on the line to destroy that monster, to defend the place he loved.

Sure, it had been dumb of Boss to do, and all the Ooawans seemed to think so as well, but the choice made sense to Magnus. In fact, it inspired him. Somewhere along the way, he had lost sight of himself. Things back in Twilight Peak were bad, sure, but part of that was because he hadn't been battling evil the way he should be. It was time to stand up. To fight for a better tomorrow.

He laughed at himself as he walked. His time from home hadn't gone quite the way he'd expected. But maybe everything was better for it.

Thank you for showing me the way, Boss, he thought. *Maybe someday I can repay you.*

Soon he reached his truck. He unlocked the front door and climbed inside. He sat for a minute to catch his breath and ease his leg, glancing over at the photo on his dash. The image featured Paige and Ryan. His heart swelled at the thought of seeing them again.

As he started the truck, one more thought struck him before he pulled off the side of the road. *I bet Ryan and Boss would be great friends.*

FATED
ENCOUNTERS

Written by:
D.R. Mills

*If you would like to follow D. R. Mills's journey or the **MONSTERS** series specifically, check out the author's official Twitter and Instagram accounts:*

Instagram: @monsters_bookseries

Twitter: @MonstersSeries

Facebook: @Monsters/100067554032850

TikTok: www.tiktok.com/@monstersseries

If you enjoyed the story, dont forget to leave a review on your preferred platform! Reviews help authors find more readers, and if you'd like D. R. Mills to be able to release books faster, reviews are the best way to support him.

CONTINUE THE STORY IN
B O O K O N E :

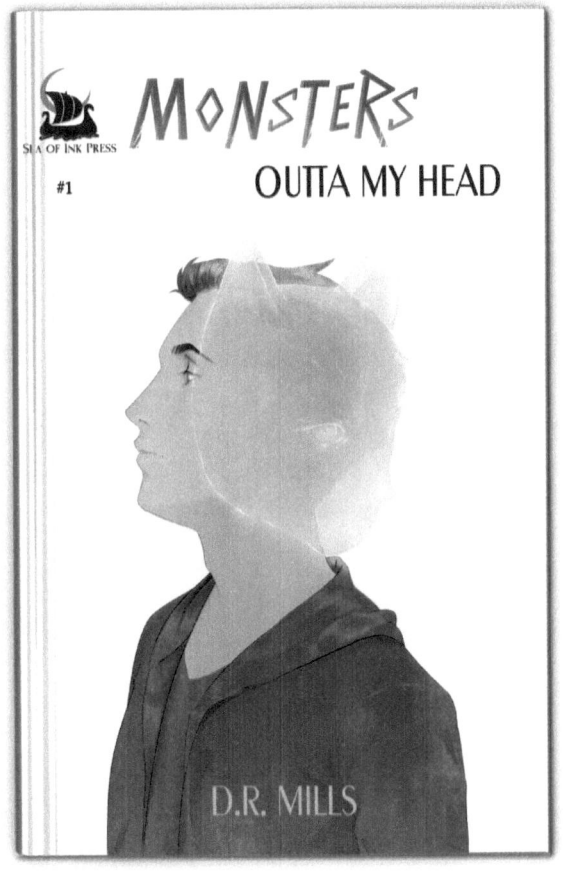

D. R. MILLS

is a young-adult horror author who is currently hard at work on his debut series, *MONSTERS*. He was born and raised in Wyoming, where he's still lurking around somewhere. When he isn't writing, he's playing video games a borderline unhealthy amount or spending time with his beautiful wife.

WWW.SEAOFINKPRESS.WORDPRESS.COM